The push of the water almost shoved Worf right past the door. But as he sailed by, his desperate fingers managed to snag the door frame.

Worf, K'Ehleyr, and the water poured into the weapons room. It filled up within seconds, but for a brief second there was air. The two Klingons expelled what they had in their lungs and greedily sucked in more, a moment before being inundated once again.

Worf angled himself around underwater. He placed his feet against one wall and then pushed off, shooting across the submerged weightlessness of his environment. He sailed across the room and locked his hands onto the heavy-duty rifle he'd been examining earlier.

Even underwater, he could see K'Ehleyr's questioning look. *What good is that going to do?* it was asking.

He wasn't exactly in a position to explain.

He only hoped that his plan worked, and that the others would survive long enough to benefit from it. . . .

Star Trek: The Next Generation
STARFLEET ACADEMY

#1 Worf's First Adventure
#2 Line of Fire
#3 Survival

Available from MINSTREL Books

STARFLEET ACADEMY™ #3
SURVIVAL

Peter David

Interior Illustrations by James Fry

A MINSTREL® BOOK

PUBLISHED BY POCKET BOOKS

New York   London   Toronto   Sydney   Tokyo   Singapore

A MINSTREL PAPERBACK *ORIGINAL*

A Minstrel Book published by
POCKET BOOKS, a division of Simon & Schuster Inc.
1230 Avenue of the Americas, New York, NY 10020

This book is published by Pocket Books, a division of Simon & Schuster Inc., under exclusive license from Paramount Pictures.

ISBN: 0-671-87086-6

First Minstrel Books printing December 1993

10 9 8 7 6 5 4 3 2 1

A MINSTREL BOOK and colophon are registered trademarks of Simon & Schuster Inc.

Cover art by Catherine Huerta

Printed in the U.S.A.

Dedicated to

Shana and Jenny, my newest
readers; Ariel, a future
reader; and Rosie, for
keeping an eye on all of them.

STARFLEET TIMELINE

2264

The launch of Captain James T. Kirk's five-year mission, U.S.S. Enterprise, NCC-1701.

2292

Alliance between the Klingon Empire and the Romulan Star Empire collapses.

2293

Colonel Worf, grandfather of Worf Rozhenko, defends Captain Kirk and Doctor McCoy at their trial for the murder of Klingon chancellor Gorkon.

Khitomer Peace Conference, Klingon Empire/Federation (Star Trek VI).

2323

Jean-Luc Picard enters Starfleet Academy's standard four-year program.

2328

The Cardassian Empire annexes the Bajoran homeworld.

2341

Data enters Starfleet Academy.

2342

Beverly Crusher (née Howard) enters Starfleet Academy Medical School, an eight-year program.

2346

Romulan massacre of Klingon outpost on Khitomer.

2351

In orbit around Bajor, the Cardassians construct a space station that they will later abandon.

2353

William T. Riker and Geordi La Forge enter Starfleet Academy.

2354

Deanna Troi enters Starfleet Academy.

2356

Tasha Yar enters Starfleet Academy.

2357

Worf Rozhenko enters Starfleet Academy.

2363

Captain Jean-Luc Picard assumes command of U.S.S. Enterprise, NCC-1701-D.

2367

Wesley Crusher enters Starfleet Academy.
An uneasy truce is signed between the Cardassians and the Federation.
Borg attack at Wolf 359; First Officer Lieutenant Commander Benjamin Sisko and his son, Jake, are among the survivors.
U.S.S. Enterprise-D defeats the Borg vessel in orbit around Earth.

2369

Commander Benjamin Sisko assumes command of Deep Space Nine in orbit over Bajor.

Source: Star Trek® Chronology / Michael Okuda and Denise Okuda

SURVIVAL

CHAPTER

1

Calling it a "city" would have been strongly exaggerating.

It was a settlement—and not much of one at that. No building was higher than two stories tall. Furthermore, much of the area lay in ruin. Most buildings had gaping holes, or no roof, or were simply rubble.

There was hardly any movement, because it was the hottest part of an already hot day, and the few inhabitants of the settlement were indoors.

The air hung heavily in the subspace communications building—a building that had been badly damaged, but nevertheless had been the first one restored to some semblance of order. There were no breezes to move through it and cool things down.

The individual who was on monitor duty did not care about such things, and wouldn't have admitted it even if he did. His skin was hard and many faceted. His eyes, nose, and mouth were little more than slits. He wore the uniform of a Starfleet cadet and the expression of someone who was growing bored and convinced his current assignment was pointless.

That did not stop him, however, from doing what he was supposed to do.

He checked the chronometer and sighed. For the past fifty-nine minutes he had been monitoring any possible subspace transmissions. None had been incoming. Now, as scheduled, he was to place his hourly call for help.

He tapped the comm padd, and then spoke slowly and carefully.

"Attention," he said. "This is Dantar IV, transmitting to any Federation or Klingon vessel. We are in distress. Repeat. We are in extreme distress. Please send representatives as soon as possible. This is a Code One emergency. Please respond or send representatives. Dantar out."

He fed the message through the encoder, scrambling it so that only those for whom it was intended would be able to make sense of it. The message had been carefully worded, hashed out in detail by the current population of Dantar IV, which had dwindled literally overnight from several hundred—a mixture of Federation and Klingon colonists—to precisely eight.

Dantar IV had been victimized by a furious and utterly unprovoked assault. The assault had been repelled and the attacker destroyed, but at a terrible cost. The colony world had been so extensively ravaged that maintaining it was impossible.

The evacuation shuttles, however, had been crammed to capacity. So eight brave individuals had volunteered to stay behind: five Starfleet Academy cadets, and three Klingon cadets. The person doing the transmitting, Zak Kebron, was one of the former.

Zak was a member of the warrior race known as the Brikar. And at that particular moment, he was reflecting on their situation.

Two weeks. Two weeks, going on three, they had been sitting on Dantar, awaiting rescue. But none had been forthcoming. When the colonists had departed, they assured the cadets that barely a week would pass before help arrived.

Not that those remaining behind were in life-threatening danger. Not yet, at any rate. Although the food-storage facilities had been devastated past the point of supporting hundreds of colonists, there was more than enough to accommodate the eight volunteers for several weeks to come.

There was shelter: a couple of buildings with four walls and a roof left standing. That was sufficient, if not the height of luxury.

But there was also the loneliness to deal with. The loneliness, and the awareness that more attacks might be forthcoming. The uncertainty of what might happen—and what might not.

What if they were there more than several weeks, and the food did, in fact, run out? What would they be reduced to doing in order to subsist? At what point was survival, simply for the sake of survival, no longer worth it?

They were difficult questions, questions to which Zak had no answers.

All he had, instead, was time. He checked the chronometer again.

The big problem was that they didn't even have any proof that the transmissions being sent were, in fact, going anywhere—at least, anywhere of significance.

A number of vital components in the subspace transmission console had been pulverized and were beyond repair. The cadets had rigged it up as best they could. But there was a very great likelihood that the signal they were sending was so weak that a receiver would practically have to be in orbit to pick it up.

What else, though, could they do?

Zak heard footsteps behind him. He almost didn't bother to turn around, but the habit of caution prompted him to do so.

He kept a neutral expression on his face as he saw a tall, fierce-looking Klingon enter. His long moustache, with small metal caps at the ends, swayed slightly from the motion of his head. Kodash.

The Klingon chucked a thumb. "I will take over," he said.

Zak knew, all too well, that Kodash had taken an immediate dislike to him. Kodash had been one of the three Klingon emissaries who had been sent to the colony world at the same time as the Federation cadets. Since Dantar IV had been a co-venture of the Federation and Klingons, representatives from both concerned groups had shown up when arguments among the colonists had threatened to destroy the colony. The representatives had managed to smooth things over. Then the unknown attackers destroyed the colony.

Now it was taking every bit of self-control that the cadets and Klingons possessed not to fall into the same trap of squabbling that had poisoned the atmosphere of the colony in the first place.

However . . .

Kodash had not been making it easy. He had made no effort to hide his disdain for Zak Kebron, just as the Brikar had traditionally taken great pride in their dislike for Klingons.

Zak knew that Kodash had legitimate reason for showing up at that particular moment. It was Kodash's time to take over monitoring the subspace communications. A schedule had been worked up, times doled out.

However . . .

It was a combination of Zak's own frustration, of Kodash's manner, of the gnawing worry that they might never get off the barren rock called Dantar IV, and the utter lack of movement in the air. All of that together prompted Zak to respond, "It's all right."

Kodash cocked his head with impatient curiosity. "What is all right?"

"I can stay on duty for a while longer." Zak waved him off dismissively. "You go attend to other matters."

Kodash strode forward.

For a satisfying moment, Zak could almost see the veins starting to stand out on the sides of Kodash's head. And then slowly, deliberately, he said, "Move— out of—the way."

Zak gave the single most effective reply he could. He turned in his chair, presenting his back to the Klingon.

Kodash snapped.

And a second later, so did the chair.

He knew better than to try and shove the Brikar out of the seat. Zak was too heavy, and the leverage was all wrong. So he chose the next best thing. The chair was mounted on a single, rather heavy, support strut. Kodash grabbed the back of the chair and yanked with all his strength. The chair snapped off, and Zak was sent tumbling to the ground.

Kodash had no time at all to gloat over this. Zak did not even fully stand up. He scrambled from his crouched position on the floor and charged forward, his legs moving like pistons. All the weeks of frustration and pent-up anger flooded out. There was far more to the outburst than just the dislike that the two had taken to each other. There was the overwhelming sense of helplessness over their situation, and the unnerving prospect that it might continue indefinitely.

Zak hurled himself at Kodash, leaping through the air, arms spread wide. Kodash barely rolled out of the way in time as Zak threw himself forward. The two stumbled out of the building into the "town" square.

Zak drew back his fist. A firm hand clamped down on Zak's wrist, stopping him from delivering the punch. A strong voice said, in no uncertain terms, "No, Zak. Do not do it."

The angry Brikar did not even look back over his shoulder. "Let go, Worf," he said.

"First you let go of Kodash," Worf replied.

Now Zak did turn to look at his fellow cadet. "This is not your concern."

The strong young Klingon did not release his grip on Zak's wrist. If anything, it grew more resolute. "Zak, this will accomplish nothing," he said.

The other cadets were approaching the square now, as were the other Klingons. They'd heard the sound of fighting, the angry voices, the crashing and the struggle. In the still air of Dantar IV, sounds had a habit of carrying rather far.

Worf gave them a glance that spoke volumes. *Let me handle this,* it said.

Kodash now had enough of his breath back to say defiantly, "He provoked it!"

"I provoked nothing," replied Zak sharply. "I spoke with respect. *You* took offense at my politeness."

"Lower your fist," said Worf, "and we will discuss this in a civil manner."

When they had first met, Zak would have trusted Worf no more than he did any other Klingon. In time, though, through continued exposure to Worf, he had come to trust in his Klingon classmate. But he had discovered that this trust did not automatically extend to other Klingons. Indeed, he was finding it singularly difficult to tolerate them, much less trust them.

Nevertheless, Zak lowered his fist.

He was aware of several of his classmates watching him. Tania Tobias, the young engineering wizard, watching through narrow, slitted eyes. Her blond hair, once kept with meticulous care, was dried out and frizzy from the relentless heat. She looked far more haggard and tired than when she had first arrived.

To her right was Mark McHenry, usually called by his nickname, "Mac." His specialty of astronavigation was of limited use when stranded for long periods of time on a deserted colony world. Mac was an airy soul, with a tendency to "zone out" on various occasions. At those times it seemed as if he were not paying attention to what was going on around him. In fact, he was hyper-aware—so much so, in fact, that he only needed to give it a small portion of his concentration. The rest was devoted to just about anything that occurred to him. At this moment even Mac was fully attuned to the stress of the moment.

While Zak's notice was on the cadets, Worf was studying the Klingons, waiting to see what their reaction to the current crisis might be.

One of the two remaining Klingons was named Gowr. The shortest of the three, he was still exceptionally formidable. He held no love for humans or Brikar, and also possessed an obvious contempt for Worf. Worf was Klingon on the outside, but Starfleet on the inside. It was a mix that Gowr considered to be completely inappropriate, and a recipe for distrust. Fortunately, however, Gowr was not in command.

That fell to the young female Klingon who labored to keep her classmates in control.

Her name was K'Ehleyr. She was stern, proud, unyielding. When she spoke it was with a confidence in her abilities and a certainty that she was always, positively, absolutely right. She had so much confidence, in fact, that the possibility that she could be wrong about anything seemed remote.

In short, K'Ehleyr was everything that any Klingon female could possibly aspire to be. Worf's respect for her had metamorphosed over the weeks from grudging admiration to grudging awe. As torn as he perpetually felt between his Klingon heritage and human upbringing, he envied her peace of mind and certainty in all things. The time they'd spent on the planet, while having clear effects on the composure and physical wellbeing of practically everyone else there, had driven K'Ehleyr into a state of utter calm.

To some degree, it worried Worf a little. It almost made him wonder if K'Ehleyr was due to crack at any time, bottling up whatever frustrations and fears she might have. And perhaps this latest altercation would be the thing that pushed her over the edge.

"Kodash, what happened?" demanded K'Ehleyr.

Kodash straightened his uniform, and said in an angry voice, "It was time for my watch on the subspace monitor. The Brikar would not yield it to me."

"Did you begin the fight or did he?"

"He began it."

"I did no such thing," said Zak firmly.

K'Ehleyr's gaze flickered to Worf. Worf folded his arms and said firmly, "If Zak Kebron states that he did not begin the fight, then that is sufficient for me."

"Are you calling me a liar?" thundered Kodash.

K'Ehleyr turned her attention back to Kodash. "Did he physically assault you first?"

"That is of no relevance."

"It is of relevance to me, Kodash," K'Ehleyr said, voice like flint. "That should be sufficient for you. Now, did the Brikar strike you first? Answer me, yes or no."

"No, but—"

"Get out of here, Kodash."

Kodash looked like he was about to erupt. "How dare you . . ."

When K'Ehleyr spoke again, her voice was lower and softer. They had all learned by this point that the angrier K'Ehleyr got, the more softly she spoke. She got good and angry without getting loud and angry. And what she said, softly and firmly, was, once again, "Get out of here, Kodash."

Kodash opened his mouth to argue once more, but then closed it. The look in K'Ehleyr's eyes, the sound of her voice, finally penetrated. He took a step back, tossed a glare once more at Zak, and then stalked away.

Worf promptly took Zak a few steps aside, and said in no uncertain terms, "You had no business provoking him in that manner."

"What's your problem, Worf?" demanded Zak. "Even K'Ehleyr took my side—"

"I am not K'Ehleyr," Worf reminded him. "And what I say is that you knew perfectly well that your actions would prompt the reaction that Kodash had. Do not cause such situations in the future. Is that understood?"

Worf and Zak had been through a great deal together. First enemies, then roommates and classmates, and finally allies. But now even the strength of that long-standing relationship was being sorely tested.

Zak seemed to consider for a long moment how to respond. And finally he settled on a simple "Yes."

"Good," said Worf. "I very much anticipate not having to have this discussion in the future. Now, if you wish continued duty in the monitor room, then do not let me stop you."

Zak nodded briefly, and headed back into the monitoring building.

Worf glanced around at the others, and said, "I would think that you all have more important things to occupy your time than to witness this display. Am I correct?"

There were brief nods from the other cadets, and then they headed back to what they had been doing.

Only at that point did Worf let out a slow breath. Of everyone who had entered the square to witness the blowup between Zak and Kodash, only Worf and K'Ehleyr remained.

They stood there in silence for a moment, a silence that K'Ehleyr eventually broke. "Well," she said briskly, "that could have been a lot worse."

"Indeed," agreed Worf. "We were fortunate."

She let out a low sigh, and for the first time in weeks Worf detected the slightest hint of uncertainty. "Worf," she said slowly, "what in the name of Kahless is going to happen to us?"

"We will be rescued," he said firmly.

"You believe that?" She took a step closer to him, and now he saw the sadness in her eyes. Clearly the confidence she exuded was not necessarily a true indicator of her genuine state of mind.

"Of course I believe it," said Worf. "Why would I believe otherwise?"

She rubbed the bridge of her nose between her thumb and forefinger. "Because we have not heard from anyone since the colonists departed in their ships. Because it is taking everything we have not to be at each other's throats. Worf—you might be deluding yourself."

"I refuse to consider that."

She shrugged her shoulders. "If you refuse to believe that the sun is hot, does that make the sun any less hot? No, I think not. The universe does not hang on your approval of its nature. It simply is what it is. Believe anything other than that, if you care to. But you would be deluding yourself. And self-delusion is a luxury that a leader cannot afford."

She turned from him and started to walk away.

Then she turned around. "At least your science expert, Soleta, did not come running out here to watch that senseless altercation. It is comforting to know that at least the Vulcan has better things to do with her time."

Worf simply nodded. No reason to mention to K'Ehleyr that Soleta had not shown up because she wasn't in the town.

Soleta had been the least affected by the arid nature of Dantar. There were two reasons for this. First, her homeworld of Vulcan was fairly arid to begin with. Her body had a variety of built-in mechanisms that enabled her to deal with the scorching environment of Dantar.

Second, the renowned Vulcan stoicism would not have permitted her to admit that she was having difficulties, even if she were.

At this moment, she was out in the desert, exploring the environment. Taking readings. Conducting experiments. In short, she was . . .

She was overdue, was what she was.

CHAPTER

The sun of Dantar beat down on Soleta, but she didn't even notice it. Her full attention was on her tricorder, which was responding with a rather puzzling "blip" reading.

She checked it once more and confirmed that it was, indeed, in working order. And what it was telling her was totally unexpected.

Her original plan involved monitoring soil samples for possible future farming use. But matters had taken a decidedly different turn, because her tricorder was unmistakably picking up some sort of signal.

"A beacon," she murmured to herself. "A homing beacon of some sort." Yes. Yes, that was definitely it.

She tapped her communicator. "Soleta to Worf," she said.

Nothing.

Her eyebrows knit together a moment and she tried again. Again there was no response.

Had the heat affected it? That seemed unlikely. Perhaps . . .

Perhaps the communication was being jammed.

Now there was an intriguing thought. Some sort of automatic homing beacon that was also serving to scramble communications by anyone who might discover it. Or, at least—and here was the part that was worrisome, were Soleta prone to worry—scrambling communications on frequencies used in Starfleet communicators.

"Fascinating," she murmured.

Soleta had two options at this point. She could return to the settlement, alert the others, and bring them back—which was the prudent and cautious thing to do—or she could stay around and investigate.

Soleta knew that going to alert the others might be the wrong move, since she had no idea what was sending the beacon. It might be coming from some installation that was permanent. On the other hand, it might be a passing vessel—someone who had landed for whatever reason, and might be taking off shortly.

It could be someone friendly, and they would be rescued.

Of course, on the other hand, it could be someone hostile, who might endeavor to kill Soleta the moment she showed up.

So many possibilities suggested themselves. But the one that preyed most on Soleta's mind was that, if she left now, she might never have the opportunity to find out. A missed chance.

It was the notion that her curiosity might not be

satisfied that was uppermost in her mind, superseding her own safety. Of what consequence was that, when one got down to it? She was stuck on a planet with lightly seasoned cadets, cranky Klingons, and dwindling chances of rescue. She was *already* in danger. It was like being out in the rain. Once you were wet, all you could get was more wet, which somehow wasn't as bad.

Soleta proceeded carefully, using as shelter the few rocks and small outcroppings that dotted the otherwise flat landscape.

She made her way over a very small mountain, and froze where she was.

It was a ship, all right, gleaming white-green metal in the sunlight. It lay on the ground, in ruins, incapable of lifting off again. Stabilizers and thrusters littered the landscape. Air foils had been torn away, and there was a fairly long skid mark along the ground—almost half a mile long, as near as Soleta could tell. The ship had come in at an angle, sliding along the ground out of control, being badly chewed up as it went.

Soleta recognized it immediately. If the markings and general shape—at least, what was left of the shape— were not sufficient for identification, certainly the huge burn marks on the hull were distinctive.

They were the kinds of scars that a ship sustained when it was hit by phaser fire, in particular, the phaser cannon that was positioned on the surface of Dantar IV.

There was no question whatsoever in Soleta's mind that she had come upon the downed ship that had at-

tacked the colony. Tricorder readings during the attack identified a ship of Klingon design, but packing Federation weaponry. This bizarre combination had caused much fury and many accusations between the two groups of colonists, as both sides had pointed fingers and accused the other of sabotage. The unresolved question of the ship's origin plagued the cadets who had been left behind.

That question could wait.

She moved forward.

She was not unprepared for trouble. For that reason, a phaser was securely attached to her belt. She checked quickly to make sure that it was fully powered up. It was.

She hoped she would not need it.

Soleta approached the ship carefully, studying the tricorder for any sign of life. There was no movement. There was no one on board—no one alive, at any rate.

But the homing beacon was still going. The question was, had it been set by someone once it had landed, which would imply that someone had survived? Or had it gone on automatically upon impact? It could have also been activated by someone who then died shortly thereafter.

So many possibilities.

She slid through one of the gaping holes, her booted feet landing noiselessly on the deck of the ship. Light cascaded through the various rips and holes in the ship's hull, which was fortunate. Although she was armed, it had not occurred to her—in the blazing light of Dantar—to carry a flashlight.

As she made her way cautiously further into the ship, though, the light decreased and the darkness surrounded her. The metal grating creaked under her weight, and every noise was magnified, sounding like thunder in the silence.

She bumped into a body.

Soleta jumped back, startled. She squinted, her eyes adjusting to the lesser light.

No, it was not a body. She aimed her tricorder at it, and came up utterly empty. Then she saw the open locker to the right, and understood. It was some sort of work suit, possibly for effecting repairs on the ship while in space. It was empty, and had fallen out of the locker when the ship had crashed.

She managed mild annoyance at having been caught off guard.

She glanced at the tricorder, and there it glared at her, a warning of perhaps half a second.

A life reading.

Directly in front of her.

Whatever it was, it had managed to approach her in total silence—no mean feat, considering the sharpness of her Vulcan hearing.

Reflexively, Soleta took a step back, and that was quite likely the only thing that saved her life.

She felt a swift movement of air directly in front of her. A swinging fist. If there had been any doubt on Soleta's part that she was dealing with a hostile entity, that notion had quickly been laid to rest.

Soleta took two more steps backward, and her attacker came after her. She dodged to the left, a furious blow missing her, and yanked out her phaser. But as she brought it up, an arm swung back, backhanding the weapon out of her grasp. It clattered away somewhere into the dimness of the ship.

She glanced in the direction that the phaser had gone, and that proved a mistake. While she was momentarily distracted, a fist lashed out. It connected with the side of her head. Stars exploded behind Soleta's eyes. She staggered, using all her strength just to stay conscious.

Her back slammed against the wall of the ship. This was a blessing, because it gave her something to brace herself against.

She reached into herself, finding the calm center,

reaching into her training and discipline. There would be no panic. There would be no rash moves. There would be no mental scolding over how she should have had people backing her up.

She was here. She was in trouble. She would handle it. That was all.

Before her attacker could move again, Soleta brought her right hand down and right knee up. She trapped his arm in between, momentarily immobilizing it. For one dangerous instant she was off-balance and vulnerable. It was a necessary gamble as her left arm stabbed out for the support she needed.

She found it: her attacker's shoulder.

The skin she felt under her fingers was leathery, and almost rock hard. It was very familiar, but she saved identification for later. Now survival was all that mattered. She squeezed hard, pressing thumb and fingers down in the manner she had been taught.

There was a startled gasp from the darkness. Her opponent staggered. That was all. Just staggered. The Vulcan nerve pinch should have rendered him instantly unconscious. Soleta pushed down harder, with all her strength.

Her enemy stumbled, and cracked his head against the wall that had been Soleta's salvation moments before. Soleta's weight was now on him, her limbs tangled in his. He pitched forward with a dull roar and Soleta went down as well, unable to extricate herself in time. They crashed to the floor with an impact that Soleta might have sworn—were she a fanciful individual—was sufficient to shake the entire planet.

For a long moment neither of them moved. Soleta's breath was coming in ragged gasps, but her attention was fully focused on her attacker.

He made no sound, didn't so much as stir.

He was out cold.

Soleta pulled herself out from under him and simply sat there for a moment, steadying her breathing. She allowed herself a small glimmer of satisfaction, but that was all. Even that was something of a luxury for a Vulcan. But she had earned it.

She rose, dusting herself off, wiping the grime and grit from her uniform. She smoothed it out as best she could, and then studied the situation before her.

What to do with him?

Space in the ship was cramped, so she simply reached around in the darkness until she found one of his legs. Then she dragged him out the same hole she'd entered through.

Her eyes adjusted very quickly to the light. Light to dark took her a while, but dark back to light was

no trouble thanks to the structure of the Vulcan eye
that provided extra protection against brightness.

She looked down at who she'd been fighting.

It was exactly what she had thought.

There was no question in her mind that someone was
going to be very upset when she got back to the
settlement.

CHAPTER

Tania and Mac were checking over the energy level of the generator that was powering the few functioning buildings. Tania glanced up when Worf walked in. He had his arms draped behind his back, just as he usually did when he made his rounds. And as he had so many times before, he rumbled, "Report?"

Tania smiled slightly. "The same as yesterday, Worf. And the same as the day before that, and the day before that. The generator is operational. The power levels are acceptable. All connections are holding solidly. There are no disruptions in any of the lines." She paused. "Did you expect me to say something else?"

He did not return her smile. "I expect that you will respond with an accurate report. Nothing more than that."

She nodded. "All right, Mr. Worf," she said simply. "I understand."

He turned on his heel, and then Tania said, "Oh—Mr. Worf."

"Yes?"

"I noticed on the way over here that K'Ehleyr was seated outside the Klingon dormitory. She seemed a bit depressed. Since you two are the respective group leaders, perhaps you might want to talk with her and find out what the problem is."

"Oh?" He seemed to consider a moment, and then continued, "Very well. Thank you for informing me of this—situation."

"Not a problem," she said.

Worf walked out.

Mac seemed very intent on studying some pulse readings, and didn't even look up as he said, "That was very nice of you."

"What was?" she asked.

"Suggesting he go over to K'Ehleyr that way. I mean, it's obvious that you're crazy about him."

Tania's jaw dropped to somewhere around her ankles. "I *beg* your pardon?"

"I said it's fairly obvious . . ."

"Yes, I know what you said."

"Then why did you ask?" He looked up at her for the first time. "Are you very forgetful?"

"Mac, I am not *crazy* about Worf."

"Really?"

"Yes. I admit I'm fond of him. He's a good friend and a fine cadet—and loyal—and . . ." She caught herself, and then said firmly, "But any sort of crush would be inappropriate and out of line."

"Really?"

"Yes, really. So stop saying that."

"Okay." Then he paused a moment. "Wait—just to make sure. Should I stop saying that you're crazy about Worf? Or should I stop saying the word 'really'? Or the word 'that'? The first I can live with. The second might be tricky. And if it's the third, then frankly, dropping the word 'that' from my vocabulary could be a bit of a prob—"

"The first two," she said quickly.

"Okay." He went back to what he was doing, and then observed, "The reason I thought it was really nice of you is because it's fairly obvious that Worf is crazy about K'Ehleyr."

"He is *not!*" She laughed, as if the very notion were absurd and had never, in a million years, occurred to her.

"Rea . . . truly?" he said.

"Yes, truly."

"Hmmm. Well, then I guess I'm completely confused."

"Why are you confused, Mac?" she asked patiently.

"Well, the way I was reading the situation, you find Worf very attractive. But you feel that he would be much happier with K'Ehleyr, and so you're going out of your way to hide your own feelings, acting in Worf's best interests. Frankly, I thought it was rather noble of you."

"Yes, well . . ." she cleared her throat. "I suppose that *if* that was what I was doing, it *would* be kind of noble of me. Not that it *is* what I'm doing, mind you."

"Whatever you say, Tania."

There was silence for a long moment, and then Tania smiled and said, "You know, Mac, I have to admit that for a guy who doesn't seem to be paying much attention to what's going on, you constantly amaze me."

He looked up. "I'm sorry. What?"

"Forget it," she said.

"All right," he replied, and ducked his head back down to work.

K'Ehleyr was precisely where Tania had said she was. She was seated just outside the building that was serving as the Klingon residence hall, on a piece of upright rubble. Worf came to a halt beside her and just stood there, his arms folded across his chest.

"Soleta is overdue," he said. "She told me the direction she was going to be exploring today. Even taking into account that it is further from the city than she has gone before, she should still have returned by now. I am planning to go in search of her."

"Do you need any help?" she asked.

"Are you volunteering?"

"Are you asking?"

"I am not asking."

"Then I am not volunteering."

There was silence between them for a moment. Worf rolled his eyes.

"If the two of us went together," Worf said, "then one of us could return to the encampment to summon help, should there be a difficulty."

"True." Again there was a pause. "Then you are asking that I come along."

"I am merely observing, out loud, the advantages."

"Very well," she said. She stood and brushed dust from the back of her clothes. "Since you require my presence—"

"I do *not*—"

"I would like to come along," she finished, sounding a bit less formal than before.

Worf did not smile, of course. That would have been inappropriate. He was, however, inwardly amused. Two Klingons—so driven by matters of pride and self-reliance that neither of them could possibly admit that he or she might need help. Or even admit to the idea that maybe, just maybe, each would like to spend some time with the other.

Nothing else would have been appropriate.

They headed in the direction that Soleta had gone, bringing with them some simple equipment such as tricorders, phasers (in the unlikely event some danger presented itself), and canteens (in the more likely event that thirst presented itself).

Occasionally Worf glanced K'Ehleyr's way, but she didn't seem particularly interested in conversing. Nevertheless, he decided to toss a question her way. "Why were you sitting outside in that manner earlier?"

"Does Starfleet recommend a different manner of sitting?" she replied.

His mouth twitched in just the slightest semblance of a smile, but he didn't let it show. "No. That was Starfleet-issue sitting."

"Good." She sighed, and before Worf could inquire further, she volunteered, "I did not wish to go in because Kodash was in there. He was rather upset, because he felt that I did not defend his position in the argument earlier."

"For what it is worth," said Worf, "I told Zak Kebron I thought he had acted poorly." He shook his head. "It is not easy for old prejudices to be put aside."

"I know," she said.

They walked for a bit more.

"It has been—rather frustrating for me," K'Ehleyr said.

"It has been frustrating for all of us."

"Not just this situation. My entire life has been frustrating."

He made no attempt to hide his surprise. "I find that difficult to believe," he said.

"You do? Why?"

"Because you seem extremely capable. Because you command respect. Because . . ."

"You do not understand, Worf."

"Then explain it to me."

She sighed. "I have human blood in my ancestry, Worf."

"You do?" He made no attempt to hide his surprise.

"Yes, I do. And I have spent every day of my life trying to ignore it, to overcome it." Her pace, which had been moving at a mile-eating clip, had slowed. "I have always pushed myself, above and beyond what any Klingon reasonably expects of him- or herself. Because I feel a need to prove myself. Prove that some—

some biological mishap does not render me unfit as a warrior, as a woman. As a Klingon." She shook her head. "I must sound ridiculous to you."

"To me? You think this could sound ridiculous to *me?* Remember to whom you are talking, K'Ehleyr. I was raised among humans. Although my parents made every attempt to honor and understand my Klingon heritage, truly I was expected to conform to human standards of behavior. It was not an expectation that made for smooth educational experiences."

"Meaning . . . ?"

"Meaning I got into many, many fights. My father said he spent more time at school as an adult then he did when he was growing up, because of all the times my teachers requested my parents come in to discuss my 'problems.' So there you were, in the Klingon Empire, a Klingon with human blood, fighting to keep up with the expectations of being a Klingon. And there was I, on Earth, a Klingon with human upbringing, fighting to keep up with the expectations of being a human. I consider that ironic."

"I think it's something of a pity, actually," said K'Ehleyr. "I wish I'd known you when I was growing up, Worf. I hate to admit it, but you might have been of great help to me."

"And you to me," he replied.

They both stopped walking and looked at each other.

Worf was certain that there was something he should say at this moment. If only he could determine what that something might be. . . .

Suddenly K'Ehleyr noticed something out of the corner of her eye. She pointed and said, "Look!"

Worf's gaze followed where she was indicating, and then he saw it, too. A lone female figure, carrying some sort of burden across her shoulders.

No. Not just a burden. A body.

"It is Soleta!" said Worf, and quickly he ran toward her. The tricorder slapped against his thigh as his powerful legs churned under him. K'Ehleyr was right behind him, keeping up admirably.

"Are you all right?" he called out as he drew within hearing range of her.

"Obviously," she replied.

"Who is that?" K'Ehleyr called out.

Soleta did not reply immediately. Instead she came to a halt and waited patiently until Worf and K'Ehleyr got there, and a moment or two more for them to catch their breath. "He is," she said when they were composed, "our former attacker. I found his ship. Then he found me. Then I found his shoulder. And that was sufficient to terminate the first meeting."

"And you carried him all this way?"

She stared at Worf piercingly. "You have a remarkable knack for stating the obvious today, Worf. Why is that?"

"Later," said Worf. "Is he human? Klingon? What?"

"Actually," Soleta admitted, "neither."

She twisted at the hip and slid the body to the ground. It rolled back, arms to either side and legs skewed.

The Klingons made no attempt to hide their shock.

As for Soleta, she had either never been surprised, or was simply too skillful at hiding it.

"The face of the enemy," she said tonelessly.

And that face belonged to a member of a very familiar race, a race whose representatives on the planet had just doubled in number.

The unconscious attacker was a Brikar.

CHAPTER

"It's a trick! I do *not* believe it!"

Zak Kebron was stalking the interior of the cadets' quarters, looking like a walking avalanche. His three-fingered fists were tightly clenched.

The other members of his immediate group surrounded him, looking sympathetic.

"Zak . . ." began Worf, for what seemed the hundredth time.

But Zak was not paying attention. He whirled on Soleta and snapped, "How could you have done this?"

Soleta's face, as always, was impassive. "I have done nothing, Zak, except my duty as a Starfleet cadet. That, and successfully fought for my life."

"What would you have preferred, Zak?" Tania asked. "That Soleta get killed so that your pride could remain intact?"

For the briefest of moments, he actually seemed to

be considering it. Then he dismissed the idea as ludicrous, of course. But the sting of the situation still remained.

"What am I supposed to do now?" he demanded, but there was a hint of pleading in his voice. "For weeks I've been at odds with the Klingon team. They've regarded every action I've taken with suspicion, and I have held them in precisely the same light. Now we find this supposed attacker, and he's one of *my* people? Not even human, but a . . ."

Then his voice trailed off as something clearly occurred to him.

"What is it, Zak?" asked Worf.

"He couldn't be Brikar!" said Zak with growing excitement. "His ship is intact!"

"It's not *intact*," Soleta said.

"I don't mean that it's not damaged," Zak said. "I mean that there shouldn't be anything left to it at all. It is standard Brikar procedure that if a Brikar pilot loses command of his ship for any reason, he is to destroy it."

"Perhaps he still hoped to repair it," Tania offered.

"But now he's been captured," shot back Zak. "And the ship is still there. That proves conclusively that he could not be Br—"

That was when it happened.

There was a sudden, massive flash of light on the horizon that immediately caught their attention, visible through the open door of the building. The cadets shielded their eyes against the intensity of it. Seconds later, the light was followed by the sound—loud, but not deafening. A self-contained explosion, but still un-questionably powerful.

Last came the wind, blowing harshly, kicking up dust and sending pebbles skittering down the deserted streets of the Dantar IV encampment.

There was silence for a time, even after the rolling thunder of the explosion had died down.

"Something like that, Zak?" asked Worf.

Zak Kebron did not reply.

Worf entered the subspace monitor building, where the Brikar prisoner had been tied up and still lay uncon-scious. Soleta had had to knock him out so forcefully to compensate for the thickness of his skin that there was a likelihood he would remain unconscious for some time more.

K'Ehleyr, Gowr, and Kodash were there as well. Worf heard them speaking in quick, guttural Klingonese as he approached. The moment he entered, however, they lapsed into silence.

The two male Klingons were regarding him with a mixture of suspicion and outright contempt. K'Ehleyr's expression was carefully guarded and neutral. By way of launching the conversation, however, she did say, "Your Soleta does good work."

"She is very efficient," Worf agreed readily.

Kodash, however, was in no mood for compliments or small talk. "One Brikar may still be unconscious," he said, "but there is no reason we should not be ques-tioning the other one."

"I presume," Worf said, "that you are referring to Starfleet Cadet Kebron."

"Of course I am!"

"He has nothing to tell you," said Worf. "He has nothing to offer in this matter, except his own anger at the behavior of one of his own people."

"For the love of Kahless, open your eyes, Worf!" roared Gowr, backing up Kodash as he always did. "Clearly it is a conspiracy! Kebron was working with him! He is—"

"He is not a suspect in this matter," Worf said flatly.

"You cannot tell me—"

"Wrong, Gowr. I can indeed tell you. And you will listen." His look included all of them. "It appears to me," Worf said slowly, choosing every word with care, "that you have been laboring under a misapprehension. I have tried, at every opportunity, to display restraint with you. I felt it important for the smooth operation of this temporary facility. I had emphasized the importance of such restraint to my classmates as well, and with the exception of the fight between Kodash and Zak, that self-control was being displayed.

"I am beginning to think, however, that my reserve has caused you to underestimate me. To underestimate all of us. To make you believe that you can address us however you wish, whenever you wish. This is not the case."

K'Ehleyr leaned back on a console, drawing up one leg and wrapping her arms around it. She looked remarkably casual, under the circumstances. "I presume there is a point you're trying to get across?" she asked.

"Two," Worf corrected. "First, I wish to make clear that we are not weak, nor are we going to shrink from a fight. Second, there is to be no harassment of Zak Kebron because of our prisoner's origin."

"But he—" began Kodash.

"No harassment," repeated Worf, every syllable dripping with barely contained anger. "No snide remarks. No insinuations. No implications. Not so much as a glance out of place. This—situation—is not of his making. He is more upset about it than anyone else involved. And you will not exacerbate this condition with crude and insensitive remarks directed at Zak Kebron. It will not be tolerated. Is that clear as well?"

There was a long, dead silence.

"Completely," said K'Ehleyr.

Gowr's head snapped around. Undoubtedly he was about to offer a protest. But then he saw the look in K'Ehleyr's eyes, and he thought better of it. Kodash remained silent.

It was at that moment that the Brikar prisoner began to stir.

Immediately the attention of all the Klingons was focused on him.

The Brikar warrior groaned, shaking his head. Clearly his neck was stiff. Automatically he tried to reach up to rub the kinks out of it, but he was unable to move his hands. This revelation caused him surprise at first. Then understanding dawned as he felt the bonds keeping his hands immobile behind him.

He roared with inarticulate rage and thrashed about. It was a rather impressive display, although it did not accomplish a single thing except to afford the Klingons some amusement.

"You might as well save your strength," K'Ehleyr told him. "Your energy will be better served answering our questions."

The Brikar looked up, noticing her for the first time. His gaze swiveled across all the Klingons, pausing in confusion when his eyes lit upon the Klingon wearing the Starfleet uniform. Obviously it was a rather odd combination.

"I will tell you nothing," said the Brikar. "Where is the Vulcan girl? I have business to settle with her."

"You are hardly in a position to settle it from down there," Worf replied easily. "Nor do you seem to understand basic bargaining technique."

"So true, Worf," K'Ehleyr put in, sounding almost sad. "Here he says he will give us nothing, while at the same time, he wants something from us."

"Oh, he will get something from us," said Worf. "Watch him while I bring the remainder of my people over here. And then, Brikar . . ." He knelt down, his face almost at the same level as the Brikar's. "Then, I assure you, you will get far more than you bargained for."

CHAPTER

The Brikar was sitting up now, having been pulled to an upright position by Gowr and Kodash. He sat there, glowering.

Staring back at him was Zak, standing a few feet away.

The others were standing nearby, watching carefully. Zak seemed to have pulled his self-control back together. He had gone from denial of the truth to such blinding fury that they were concerned for a time that he might kill the prisoner if he got within range. Now, though, a calm had settled over him, a dangerous calm, in Worf's opinion. It was almost easier to manage the Brikar cadet when he was raging. Now, he was a smoldering volcano, apparently ready to blow at any moment.

"Who are you?" Zak interrogated.

The Brikar said nothing.

Zak repeated the question, this time in the native language of the Brikar. Still the prisoner said nothing. Zak switched back to Standard and this time, said, "I am Zak Kebron, of the Clan Kebron. Of what clan are you?"

Nothing.

"I am making a formal interrogation of your rank and status in Brikar society," Zak said. "To refuse answer is to risk immediate death challenge."

"So challenge me," said the Brikar prisoner defiantly. "Kill me, if you can. You'll be no closer to your answers than you were before, and at least I won't have to listen to the whining of some Federation tool who pretends he's a true Brikar."

Worf glanced quickly to Zak. Zak was immobile. It was as if the words had passed right through him.

"You are a terrorist," said Zak after a moment. "A terrorist and an independent operator. A disgrace to the Brikar."

"If you are waiting for me to confirm or deny your opinion, you will have to wait a very long time," shot back the Brikar. "Your insults are so much air, Kebron. You are beneath my notice." His large head swiveled to take in Soleta. "You, on the other hand, Vulcan, there will be a reckoning between us. I assure you, I never forget."

"Most elephants never do," Tania put in tartly.

Worf stepped back, assessing the situation. He gestured to K'Ehleyr, who joined him, and they turned away from the Brikar.

"The Brikar appears determined not to cooperate," observed Worf.

"This is not a surprise."

Suddenly they heard a crash behind them. They spun. Soleta, Tania, and Kodash were doing everything they could to pull Zak away from the prisoner. The prisoner was on the ground, having been kicked over by an enraged Zak. "You dare call me traitor! You are the traitor!" shouted Zak Kebron.

"I am what I am, Kebron!" shot back the Brikar prisoner from the ground. "Not some fake like you!"

Soleta was doing her best to calm Zak down. She brought him over to a corner, whispering to him intently. He kept trying to look back at the fallen Brikar, who was at that moment being brought back to upright position in his chair by Gowr and Mac. But Soleta, with firm hands, brought his face back to look at hers.

"Listen to me, Worf," said K'Ehleyr, low and intense. "I know what you will say. But it is madness to proceed in this manner. Let myself, Gowr, and Kodash have an hour alone with him."

"No."

"Half an hour, then." Her teeth flashed. "We will find out everything he knows. He will beg to tell us whatever we need."

"No," he repeated more firmly.

"Well, what would you do, then, Worf?" Clearly she was running out of tolerance for the situation. "Sit here in this manner until he becomes bored enough to give us the information? Blast it, Worf," and her voice was starting to get louder. "If he had his way, the Vulcan would be dead! Given the opportunity, he would make certain the rest of us joined her! The creature deserves no special treatment. Why are you coddling him? What sort of Klingon are you?''

"I," he said hotly, not caring if others were staring, "am a Starfleet cadet. My fellow cadets have designated me the group leader. I will not sanction torture of a prisoner. Not as long as any other means presents itself."

"There is no other means."

To their mild surprise, Mac stepped in between them. In as low a voice as possible, he said, "A cunning plan."

Worf looked at him hopefully. "Yes?"

Mac nodded firmly. "A plan so cunning, you could stick a tail on it and call it a weasel."

"And that would be . . . ?" prompted K'Ehleyr.

"That what would be?" asked Mac.

Worf was trying not to lose his patience. "The cunning plan. What is it?"

Mac chucked a thumb toward Soleta. "She can do it. Soleta can."

"Do what?"

"Vulcan mind meld. Soleta's very adept with basic mind brushes. That's why she's so good with calming people down, making them feel better. Mind brush is only one step below a full mind meld. She can do it."

Worf and K'Ehleyr looked at each other, and then back at Mac. "Since when did you become an expert on Vulcan mind techniques?"

"I read a paper on it three years ago." He frowned,

and scratched his chin. "Or maybe I wrote it. Let me think. . . ."

"Never mind. Soleta!" Worf called over to her.

"I know what you are going to ask," said Soleta, approaching them slowly. "I overheard Mac's—suggestion." Her glance flickered to Mac, and although her face was as impassive as always, she did not look particularly appreciative. "Worf, I would prefer another option."

"I am open to suggestions," said Worf. "It is K'Ehleyr's thought that we simply resort to torture. Do you consider that to be acceptable?"

She stared at him for a moment, and then—surprisingly—lowered her gaze. "That is an unnecessary question. You know that, philosophically, I would consider such actions to be repugnant."

"Soleta, I would not force you . . ."

She looked back up at him, her eyes hard and uncompromising. "You could not. Were you commander of a starship and I your subordinate, such an order would still overstep the bounds of propriety."

Worf said nothing.

Soleta seemed to be staring deep into herself. Normally Soleta had no trouble expressing herself, but in this case she was clearly having difficulty finding the words. "The Vulcan mind meld—is not an easy technique to master. It takes many, many years of practice. My teachers on Vulcan, I will admit, consider me to be something of a prodigy. They say I have a natural affinity for it. Nevertheless, I am not entirely—comfortable

45

in my abilities. And with the mind meld, the state of mind of the initiator is crucial.''

"Are you afraid?'' There was no challenge in Worf's voice.

"Afraid?'' She shook her head. "Of course not.''

"We forgot,'' said K'Ehleyr, sounding just a touch sarcastic. "Vulcans do not burden themselves with such petty concerns as fear.''

Soleta replied without looking at her. "Lack of fear is one thing, K'Ehleyr. That does not mean, however, that I am bereft of concern for self-preservation. The ideal situation for a mind meld is when both participants are willing. It is a method of communion. Using a mind meld for interrogation is like using a hammer to crack someone's skull. It can be done, but that was not the original design of the tool, and the consequences can be dire for both parties. The Brikar is a strong, fierce personality. An accomplished melder could do what you desire, but it would be difficult. For myself, a novice . . .''

And now she did turn and look at K'Ehleyr. "If I try to mind meld and extract information, I am putting myself at great risk and corrupting the intended use of the meld. If, on the other hand, I turn away and allow you to beat information out of him, I am a party to brutality. That is the choice you would have me make. I want you to understand that. I want both of you to understand.''

Worf simply nodded. There was nothing else that he could say.

CHAPTER

Soleta steepled her fingers, peering over the tops of them at the glowering face of the Brikar. She closed her eyes, as if she hoped that the answer was written on the inside of her lids. Then she let out a slow, steady breath.

When she looked at the Brikar once more, there was something in her eyes that he most definitely did not like.

"Keep her away from me," he said fiercely.

Soleta either did not hear him, or just did not care. She approached him slowly, tentatively, as if she were sizing him up. The Brikar had no clue as to what was happening. He looked from the Klingons to the cadets and then back to Soleta. "I said keep her away!"

The Vulcan seemed to be drawing into herself. Her breathing was slowing down. Her attention was now fully focused on the Brikar.

"Tell us what we want to know, Brikar," said Worf.

"Drop dead."

Soleta was now inches away from him. The Brikar looked up at her uncertainly. "I'm not afraid of you, Vulcan!" he said, rather unconvincingly.

Her hands stretched out toward his face, her fingers wide apart. Her eyes were no longer focused on his face. Instead they now seemed trained on a place somewhere in the back of his skull, as if she were looking right through him.

The Brikar was tightly bound, hand and foot, to the heavy-duty chair. The cords were molecularly dense, used as strapping to move heavy equipment. He strained against them, but was unable to break them. "Get her away from me!" he shouted.

But his gaze was locked with hers. His eyes were blazing. Hers were implacable. He tried to drive her away with the force of his stare, but there was no way that was going to work.

Soleta brought her hands up, brushing against his face. He jumped slightly, as if she had electric probes in her fingers. He tried to draw away from her, but he was unable to lean away even the least amount, a helpless victim of Soleta's penetrating scrutiny.

Very softly, so softly she could barely be heard, she whispered, "Our minds are merging . . ."

His mouth was moving. He was trying to say "No," but no words were coming out.

"Your thoughts are mine," intoned Soleta. "Your thoughts are mine. What you know, I know."

The Brikar's eyes were so wide that Worf thought they were going to leap out of his face.

"I am—Soleta," she said. With her fingers spread across his face, she pushed her mind forward, encountering barriers and trying to shove her way past them. She had to establish her presence in his mind before she could learn what she needed to know. She had to proceed carefully. "I am Soleta. I am . . ."

"So . . . Soleta," the Brikar said.

"I am Soleta." Both of them had said it together, and then she took it one step further. "We are—Soleta. We are Soleta."

He tried to resist, but it only took a moment more for him to be droning, in tandem with her, "We are Soleta."

"We are . . ." This time, she did not complete the sentence. Clearly she was waiting for him to provide his name. "We are . . ." she repeated steadily.

"Soleta," Mark McHenry prompted from nearby. Tania gestured for him to be quiet.

The Brikar was resisting, but Soleta—once embarked upon her course—would not be turned away. "We— *are—*"

He resisted for one last moment, and then the name exploded out of him. *"We are Baan,"* he gasped.

Soleta sagged a moment. The divining of this relatively small piece of information seemed to have exhausted her. But then she gathered her resources, and pushed forward. Her fingers were inflexible. It looked now as if nothing less than snapping them off would get

her to release her grip on the Brikar, whom they now knew to be named Baan.

Her voice was unrelenting. "We came to Dantar because . . ."

"We came—with a—mission," he said. Although his eyes were wide open, he wasn't looking at anyone in the room.

"And the mission was . . . ?"

His mouth twitched.

"And the mission was . . . ?" Soleta repeated. It was an indicator of the strain she was under, because she actually sounded emotional when she said it.

"Hidden—base—"

Worf's breath caught upon hearing those words. He looked at K'Ehleyr, who was likewise amazed. "Ask him where!" Worf demanded.

But Soleta didn't acknowledge the order. It was quite likely that she hadn't heard it at all. "Why?" she was asking. "Why the attacks? Why . . ."

And then she began to answer herself. Her fingers, stiff as nails, were beginning to tremble. Her eyes were closed so tightly that tears were running down the sides of her face. When she spoke again, her voice had taken on some of the graveled tone of the Brikar. As for Baan, his mouth was forming the words, but all the voice was coming out of Soleta.

"The Brikar—want unlimited—expansion privileges—" Soleta-Baan said. "Threaten—to—break off—from Federation—years of planning—established—established . . ."

Soleta stopped, then took a deep breath that seemed

to cause her so much pain that she cried out. Worf started forward to put an end to it, but Tania and Mac stopped him, taking him by either arm.

"I wouldn't advise it," said Mac.

Tania was nodding. "Yank her out of it now, it could be dangerous. Like a diver being brought up too fast from the deep. She could get the mental equivalent of the bends."

Worf looked from them to Soleta.

Soleta practically shouted the word "established," as if it were a jam that she were trying to punch past. "Established . . ." And then it came out in a rush. "Established—hidden bases within range of Federation borders. Main one on Dantar IV—way in is—is . . ."

Her body started to convulse with the strain, and she screamed. It was a terrifying thing to hear, the controlled, calm Soleta crying out as if her soul were being wrenched from her body.

It was enough for Worf. He tore loose from his classmates, ran to Soleta, and yanked her away from the Brikar. Her arms remained rigid, her fingers outstretched. She gave no sign that she knew contact had been broken.

"She's not breathing! Her breathing's stopped!" Zak Kebron shouted.

And it had. She was utterly paralyzed, as if her body had simply shut down.

Worf lay her down, tilting her head back to clear the passage to her lungs.

The Brikar, in the meantime, began to regain some semblance of normality. Understanding started to return to his eyes, and it seemed as if he were awaking from a deep dream.

Worf started to lean down to Soleta, then realized her eyes were focused on him.

"Worf—" she said slowly.

"I—you had stopped breathing—"

"I was in a trance, Worf," she informed him. "I was breathing, but at a much slower rate than normal. It was in order to bring myself gradually out of the mind meld. Such things cannot be flipped on and off like a switch."

"Oh," was all he could think of to say.

"Would you be good enough to help me up?"

He backed up, took Soleta by the hand, and brought her to her feet. She brought her hands up to her face to compose herself, and felt the wetness on her cheeks. She did an excellent job of covering the surprise she felt upon discovering it. "I was not—crying," she asked uncertainly.

Tania shook her head. "Just reflex. Your eyes were squeezed so tightly that it activated your tear ducts. Just a biological thing. Nothing, you know, emotional."

Soleta nodded, as if she had known all along that this would be the case. "I had no doubt."

With Soleta's welfare attended to, their concentration switched to their prisoner.

Baan looked up at the scowling faces of Worf, Zak, and the others, but there was a lot less of the earlier defiance in his expression.

Zak was the first to break the silence. "Greetings, Baan. How nice to know who we're talking to."

"You have told us much of what we need to know," said Worf. "The only question that remains is, how easily do you wish matters to go for you?"

"Why does that make any difference to you?" sneered Baan. But there was a lack of certainty in his behavior, and it made Worf suspect that Baan had only the haziest recollection of what had just occurred.

At the moment, Baan was off-balance and vulnerable. Now was the time to try and pry the rest out of him.

"It does not make a difference to me," Worf said, sounding utterly casual. "After all, we now know of the hidden base, and your attempts to get to it. We know of your mission to get rid of the colonists, either by driving them away or simply killing them, to gain access to the base."

Worf was guessing, of course, basing his conjectures on what they already knew and building upon it. Baan, however, did not know that. And his expression of total shock was enough to confirm to Worf that the guesses were correct.

He pressed the advantage. "Now you can tell us the rest voluntarily, if you wish. Or else we will simply turn Soleta loose on you again."

This was a complete bluff. Worf had already resolved that there was simply no way he was going to subject his Vulcan classmate to that sort of stress again. But Baan did not know that.

Nor, for that matter, did Soleta. She was, however, Vulcan, and consequently was quite expert in keeping her feelings to herself. Her face was expressionless. She looked perfectly capable of once more forcing herself into the Brikar's mind and extracting, like a dentist, the information she desired.

Worf leaned in closer, until his face was mere inches away from Baan's. He indicated Soleta with a tilt of his head.

"Will you speak before I unleash her on you once more? Because if you do not, we will still obtain the information we desire. And you will be left with as much mental agility as a potted plant. It is your decision, Baan of the Brikar. Make it carefully."

Brikar did not sweat. But if they did, then Baan would have been sweating buckets at that moment.

Worf shrugged his shoulders. "Very well. Soleta?"

He gestured for her to come forward. She did not hesitate, approaching Baan with her fingers outstretched. She looked as if she were capable of simply reaching into his head, scooping out his brains and examining them.

"All right!" shouted Baan. "All right! Just keep her away!"

Worf put up a hand, stopping Soleta in her place. "Soleta, it will not be necessary."

To Worf's surprise, she actually managed to put on an air of bitter disappointment. "Are you sure?" she asked, sounding brittle.

"For the moment."

She played it to the hilt. "You should not tease me, Mr. Worf. You know that my sources of genuine pleasure are few. And I have not drained anyone of everything they know in *such* a long time."

Vulcans did not lie. Nor had Soleta lied now. There

was, in fact, not all that much that made her happy, for "pleasure" was too strong a word to use when it came to Vulcans. "Fulfillment" might be the strongest. And since Soleta had, in fact, *never* drained anyone of everything they knew, saying that it had been a long time was the slightest stretch of the truth.

But she had spoken in such deadly earnest tones that the Brikar was visibly trembling. This was in stark contrast to Tania, who was standing behind Baan, out of sight. She had her mouth covered, her shoulders shaking in amusement. Mark McHenry, who had not fully caught on, was gaping at Soleta in astonishment. Zak had his back turned, and it was not possible to see his reaction.

Worf, poker-faced, played along. "If he does not fully cooperate, I shall permit you to—" he paused, searching for the right words—"to have your way with him."

"Thank you, Mr. Worf," she said. She bowed slightly at the waist and stepped back.

"I will cooperate, I promise you," said the Brikar wholeheartedly.

"Good." Worf folded his arms and waited.

The Brikar sighed. "Everything you've said is true. My mission was to try and drive the colonists off the planet. My ship was specially designed, using Klingon design but Federation weaponry. We wished to be rid of the colonists in whatever way we could. Whether it be through causing divisiveness between them, or rendering the planet inhabitable, it made little difference. We did *not*, wish, however, to launch an all-out attack, for fear of drawing the full attention of the Federation to our activities before we were ready.

"Yes, there is a hidden base. At the time we established it here, the colony did not exist. That was a relatively recent development. Since this part of Dantar is one of the more habitable, it was natural for us to build our base here, and just as natural, unfortunately, for the colonists to establish their colony here as well.

"The entrance to the base is hidden beneath the building in which the colony's central generators are housed. I tried to keep damage to that structure to a minimum in my attacks. Unfortunately, the entrance is only accessible by means of a signaling device that was in my ship, a device destroyed when I crashed. I had been endeavoring to repair it, although with little success. That, and to survive as best I could. But after several days, with the device still unrepaired and my supplies running low, I signaled for help. That was when"— and he paused, looking distastefully at Soleta—"that was when *she* showed up."

"This base," said Worf. "What is in there?"

"Weaponry, mostly. Everything needed to establish Dantar IV as a strategic military point, particularly for guerilla operations."

"And subspace transmission equipment?"

"Of course," said Baan, sounding a bit scornful.

"How powerful?"

"Extremely. You could bounce a signal off the Andromeda galaxy if you wanted to."

"We could summon help," Tania said in a low voice.

"Beam an emergency message straight into the heart of Federation territory."

Worf nodded, stroking his chin. "How do we gain access?"

Baan regarded him with a flickering of his old contempt. "Are you deaf, Klingon? I told you already: via a signaling device that is no longer operational."

Now Tania stepped forward. "How does—how did it operate?"

"A varying scale of tonal frequencies, set to a pre-established code."

"Do you know what the code is?"

Baan shook his head. "No, but if you want, I can bring you to the entrance. If you wish, I will even accompany you inside."

Worf looked at him suspiciously. "You seem rather eager to be of help all of a sudden."

"I have no more desire to spend the rest of my days here than you do."

Again Worf seemed to consider him. "What happened to the colonists?"

"They left." Baan looked at him oddly. "You were there. You saw it yourself."

"But rescue vessels should have been sent by now. That has not been the case. So what happened to them? Do you have any suspicions?"

"Suspicions? I suspect they fell into a black hole. I suspect they were sliced to ribbons by a cosmic string fragment. I suspect their engines ruptured. I suspect they were intercepted by Romulans. I suspect many things, Klingon. Of what possible use are suspicions?

The fact is that I have no more idea of their fate than you do. If that was not the answer that you desired to receive, then that is much more your problem than mine.''

"Indeed. That being the case, Baan, I believe that you will stay here for a time. Once we have managed to enter the hidden base, summon help, and ensure our rescue, you will be released.''

"You're a fool!'' snapped Baan. "You'll never get in there without my help! It's insanity to reject my offer of help!''

Worf's lips thinned. "If that was not the answer that you desired to receive, then that is much more your problem than mine.''

The Brikar snarled upon hearing that.

As if Baan's presence were no longer of any consequence, Worf gestured for the others to follow him out the door. K'Ehleyr assigned Gowr to keep an eye on the Brikar, and moments later everyone else was standing outside the building. Some of them were barely able to contain their excitement.

"What a coup!'' Tania practically crowed. "If we can find this hidden base of theirs, then all of this will have been worth it!''

"Do not get too excited,'' Worf cautioned her. "First, we have to find the base. Second, we have to be able to get in.''

"I wouldn't be too concerned about that,'' Tania replied. "All this time that we've been sitting around here, we've been going out of our minds because of our inability to accomplish anything. Well, that's changed. This is exactly the type of challenge we need.''

"Get on it, then," said Worf.

She tossed off a salute, a rather tongue-in-cheek maneuver since salutes were hardly required in Starfleet. She gestured for Mark to follow her, and they headed off toward the building where Tania had been doing most of her engineering work.

Worf turned to Soleta. "Are you all right?" he asked. Without Baan around, there was no need for him to disguise his concern.

She nodded. "I am—recovered," she said carefully. "Do not concern yourself, Worf. It was not one of the more pleasant experiences of my life, and I have no overwhelming urge to repeat it. But I shall survive intact."

"I had no doubt," he replied.

Zak Kebron, for his part, was standing off to the side. He was paying only partial attention to what was being said, for his mind was in turmoil over their recent discoveries. When Worf stepped up to him, Zak did not look as if he were particularly relishing the coming conversation.

"All these things that Baan said, about growing hostility toward the Federation . . ." Worf began carefully.

Having no patience for dancing around difficulties, Zak said bluntly, "You wish to know if they are true. And if they are true, you wish to know why I have said nothing of them before this."

Worf nodded.

Zak sighed. He noticed K'Ehleyr and Kodash standing nearby, within earshot. He could have tried to chase them away, take out his frustration on them. But what possible purpose would that serve?

"There had been talk," he said. "But Worf, you must understand. My people like to talk, very loudly, about a great many things. There had been anti-Federation sentiment expressed, yes. Also anti-Klingon, anti-Romulan, and on and on. The Brikar are somewhat aggressive, and not exactly pioneers in tolerant race relations. That much you must certainly know by now."

"It had come to my attention," Worf said drily.

"That being the case," continued Zak, "I had no way of knowing that sentiment would take this sort of shape. No way of knowing that *anything* would come from it, let alone hidden bases and such."

Now K'Ehleyr stepped forward. "Nevertheless, you do realize it puts you in a precarious position, security-wise."

Worf looked at her. "Oh really?"

"Yes, really. He is a member of a race known to be hostile."

"What are you suggesting?" demanded Zak, bristling. "That I should be made prisoner alongside Baan? Would that serve your ends?"

"I am simply pointing out—"

"What we already know," Worf cut her off. "You are *not* seriously suggesting that one member of the Brikar be penalized because of the actions of another?"

"No," said K'Ehleyr evenly. "I am not. I have made my observations, and have done my duty by stating them. If you feel that he is trustworthy, then your opinion as leader of your team must take precedence."

"Thank you," he said. He turned to Kodash. "And do you have anything you wish to contribute to this discussion?"

For a moment, Kodash said nothing. Zak braced himself, prepared for an outpouring of verbal abuse. Worse, he was certain that the Klingon would start gloating over the fact that not only had Zak been wrong about the attacker's being Klingon, but that it was in fact one of Zak's own people who had assaulted them. It was none other than a Brikar who had made them prisoners on Dantar IV.

Kodash was undoubtedly going to rub it in, and there was nothing that Zak could do to contradict such sentiments.

Zak waited.

"You must feel greatly humiliated that it was one of your own people who attacked us," Kodash said.

Zak said nothing.

Kodash glanced briefly at Worf, and then looked back to Zak. "I know how I would feel, were I in your position. I am glad that I am not."

Then he turned and walked away.

Zak couldn't believe it. That was it? The whole confrontation? He looked to Worf in amazement.

"I thought that was heartfelt. Did you not think so?" Worf asked.

CHAPTER 7

The cadets had never had any reason for doing a tricorder survey of the inside of the generator building. But they certainly had one now.

Mark McHenry moved carefully across the room, like an old-time water prospector with a divining rod. He was studying the tricorder readings carefully.

The entire colony had been shut down, and the generators turned off so as not to interfere. The key was to try to detect some sort of accelerated energy readings, because wherever those readings were coming from, that would be the hidden base.

The others were watching him carefully. Not a word was being spoken, nor had one been breathed in the past five minutes.

Finally Mark nodded.

"There's something around here, all right," he said slowly. "It's well shielded. But I think I've got a lock on it. Hold on."

He made his way slowly through the room, holding his tricorder out in front of him like a shield. Finally he stopped in front of the largest of the pulse generators.

"Well?" said Worf.

McHenry pointed straight down, to the base of the generator.

There were low moans from the others. "You *are* joking," said K'Ehleyr.

A frown creased McHenry's face. "I don't *think* I am. Did I say something that made you want to laugh?"

Tania rubbed her temples. "Nooo, Mac. Nothing." She looked to Worf. "Zak recently helped me move something like this, but it was about half the size of this one."

Zak stepped forward, cracking his knuckles. He did each one separately, and each one made a sound like a cannon shot. And as he engaged in this rather pointless activity, he said confidently, "Then I guess I will have to work twice as hard, won't I?"

When the generators had first been installed, high-capacity haulers had been utilized to get things around. All such convenience devices, however, had been destroyed in the raid. This did nothing to deter Zak Kebron, however, who moved over to the huge, cylindrical generator.

"Are you certain you do not need assistance?" asked Worf.

"Not a problem," said Zak with utter confidence.

He stepped up to face the generator, and wrapped his arms around it as far as they would go. He tried to lift it straight up and out of its receptacle.

It did not budge.

"Might I suggest leverage," said Worf. Ideally, what he should have done at that moment was step forward and help, whether Zak wanted it or not. But he was keenly aware of the sense of pride that Zak felt in moments such as these. Zak Kebron wasn't simply interested in moving the generator. He also wanted to show that *he was capable of doing it*.

Zak grunted once in acknowledgment, and then turned around, presenting his back to the generator. He reached around, gripping it firmly, and tried to hoist it onto his back.

There was the slightest groan of metal on metal, and then the generator started to move. Zak gritted his teeth. Now that he had gotten the thing moving, he did not want to do anything that might cause him to lose momentum.

His body was trembling under the strain, his mouth clamped shut to prevent the slightest hint of exertion from escaping his lips.

The generator moved a bit more, and then more.

Then he started to stagger. The generator began to slide out of his grasp.

Worf started toward Zak to help brace him, but Kodash was already in motion. He came up to Zak's side and threw his full weight against the generator.

It was just enough time for Zak to get a firmer grip on the generator. Kodash did not move away, but stayed next to him, helping him to steady it.

Just to play it safe, Worf came up on the other side. This, as it turned out, was fortunate, because at that moment the generator started to teeter, ever so slightly, to the other side. With Worf there, however, it did not go far at all.

They stood there for a moment, the Brikar acting as the main muscle, with the Klingons on either side, acting as spotters and supplemental muscle.

Zak glanced from one to the other. And then, very grudgingly, he muttered, "Thanks."

"You are welcome," said Kodash diplomatically. Then he fired a look at Worf that seemed to say, *See? I can be polite when I have to be.*

They took another moment to make sure that the generator was steadied on Zak's back. Then the mighty Brikar took several steps forward. Worf and Kodash stayed to either side of him, making sure that the generator did not tumble off. The other cadets and Klingons wisely stepped back. No one wanted to be nearby should the entire thing come crashing down.

"Careful," said Worf.

"I'm—*being*—careful," grunted Zak.

He started to bend at the knees, and then eased the apparatus off his back. It hit the floor with a *klang* that reverberated throughout the room.

"Excellent job, Zak," said Worf.

Kodash wasn't quite as amiable, but nevertheless he nodded in grudging acknowledgment of an impressive display of strength.

"Thank you," said Zak. And then he nodded deferentially in the direction of Kodash and repeated, "Thank you."

Mark McHenry, meanwhile, wasted no time. He

stepped into the area vacated by the generator and studied his tricorder readings. "Here," he said. "Definitely. Right here."

Beneath his feet was solid metal. Worf took a place next to him and said, "Are you sure?"

"Positive. Absolutely. Absolutely, positively sure about . . ." He paused, and frowned.

"About the hidden base," Tania prompted.

"*Yes!* Yes, absolutely sure. The hidden base is right here." He considered it a moment. "I guess we'll have to stop calling it a hidden base, huh? I mean, since we've found it and all. We'll have to start calling it the found base."

"You do that," said Worf. "Tania, open it up."

Tania was ready, armed with a laser torch. She crouched down in the area Mac had indicated, and activated the torch. She had it on the lowest possible setting, because the last thing she wanted to do was risk slicing through something that they might need later on.

She activated the torch. The pencil-thin beam lanced out, and she brought it down over the metal. There was a high-pitched whine as the beam sliced into the gleaming surface.

Tania moved it slowly, prepared to shut it off if there was something that provided the least amount of resistance. Nothing did, however. It slid through with no problem, and within minutes Tania had created a circle in the metal approximately four feet in diameter. More than enough room for anyone to get through—provided that there was anything for them to get through to.

Worf stepped in with a crowbar and, seconds later,

had levered a portion of the metal circle up. It only took him moments more to pry up the entire circle. He leaned over and looked down into the hole, as did the others.

What they saw was a short drop of several feet to a small array of blinking lights, indicating a control panel of some sort. It was mounted on what appeared to be a large metal door that was inset flat into the ground. It was round and seamless.

"That's it," breathed Tania.

"A phaser will make short work of it," Worf rumbled.

But Soleta was shaking her head. "That would not be advisable."

"Why not?" he demanded.

"Because," she said calmly, "there is every possibility that the hidden base—"

"Found base," Mac corrected.

She ignored him, and continued, "—might have some sort of failsafes built into it. If our means of entry is too violent, it could trigger some sort of self-destruct sequence. Then we would be left with nothing. Worse, if the self-destruct is sufficiently violent, we would be left in pieces."

"So we must proceed with caution," said Worf.

"Always advisable," Soleta nodded.

"Very well. Tania . . ."

"I'm already on it," she said. "Mac, give me the tricorder."

"For good? Or is this just a loan?" he asked.

"A loan."

"Okay." He handed it to her, relieved by her assurances that he would be getting the tricorder back.

Tania leaned over the hole, adjusting the tricorder. "Okay, this should work," she said, tapping some controls on the tricorder. And seconds later, it emitted a single high-pitched tone.

Soleta clapped her hands over her ears and took several steps back, finding the noise to be almost painful. Worf said, "What are you doing?"

"I think I recognize the technology they've got in use here," said Tania. "I can crack this. The tricorder is generating what's called a 'handshake signal.' It's letting the lock know that another electronic device wants to interface with it. It's the method a tricorder uses to download and upload information from computer systems."

"Are you getting anything?" Mac asked.

"Not so far. Let me shift the frequency a hair."

She made an adjustment, and there was a fractional change in the tone of the signal. When this didn't seem to generate a response, she tried again, and again . . .

And on the fifth wave frequency, she hit it.

The lights on the doorway flickered to life. A series of high-pitched signals began to sound, and a burst of information shot through the tricorder.

Reflexively, Worf braced himself against the possibility that he might be blown apart at any moment. But it didn't happen. Instead, after about thirty seconds, the sounds died down, and Tania shut off the tricorder.

"Got it," she said.

"The entry code?"

"No," she admitted. "But I have the array of signals that they use as a means of encoding. It's like having to crack a combination lock that has a hundred numbers on it, and you learn that all the numbers in the combination are actually between one and ten. You've still got your work cut out for you, but it's been whittled down quite a bit."

"So now what?" asked K'Ehleyr.

Tania allowed herself to experience a moment of superiority to the Klingon female. It was a pleasant feeling. "Now," she said, "you give me about an hour to rig up a communicator and tie it in with the tricorder, then we might just have the opportunity to get off this rock."

"You can do it, Tania," said Worf. "I have every confidence in you."

"Thank you, Worf. I appreciate that."

CHAPTER

"This is an insult!" snarled Gowr. "I should be included in this!"

He was standing in the subspace transmission room, several feet away from the tied-up Baan. He was pointing at Baan and clearly quite angry.

"Why am *I* chosen to stand guard over him?" he demanded. "Get one of the Starfleet fools to do it! If there is potential danger within the base—"

"My greatest concern about potential danger," said K'Ehleyr, "is that the prisoner might escape. If that should come to pass, we would face no end of difficulty."

"I'm not going to escape," said Baan. "Where would I go?"

"You hear?" Gowr said loudly. "He says he is not going to escape!"

"And you *believe* him?" She shook her head. "Gowr, of course he will try to escape."

"Have Kodash watch him! Or yourself!"

"Gowr, I have designated this your job for one reason, and one reason only." She clapped a hand on his shoulder. "I trust only you."

He looked at her askance. "What?"

"I do not give you this assignment lightly," she said. "If you wish to view it as some sort of 'busy work,' I cannot stop you from doing so. In my view, however, I am simply giving an important job to someone whom I feel can do it. Now is that acceptable to you or not?"

Gowr sighed, knowing that he'd been outmaneuvered. "Whatever you say, K'Ehleyr."

"Good," she said. She headed for the door, stopped and said once more, "We are counting on you, Gowr."

"Yes, yes," he replied, waving dismissively. "I shall attend to it."

And the moment that Gowr's back was turned, Baan returned to what he had been doing before. Namely, he applied slow, steady pressure to his bonds. Stretching the molecules apart, little by little, getting a bit of slack into his restraints.

Waiting for the right opportunity to make his move. . . .

CHAPTER

The back of the communicator's circuit board was open, and small connections had been made to the tricorder. And now the communicator was emitting a series of high-pitched noises and squeaks, and had been doing so for quite some time.

The Klingons and Starfleet cadets were seated or standing at various places in the room, trying not to look bored and not succeeding terribly well.

Tania seemed unperturbed. She carefully monitored the signals being transmitted through the communicator, checking it against the information being generated by the tricorder.

Finally, Zak Kebron could take it no longer. "Tania, we're wasting our time."

She didn't even bother to look back at him. "Is your vast experience in engineering telling you that, Zak? Or is it just that you're impatient?"

"I do not understand," K'Ehleyr said. "You said you could open this door."

"Tania knows what she is doing," Worf said firmly. He was not entirely sure how firmly he held that conviction himself, but nevertheless he felt it was important to present a united front. "I have every confidence in her."

"Thank you, Worf," said Tania, wondering just how honest he was being and suspecting she wouldn't like the answer. "What's happening at the moment, in case any more of you are confused," continued Tania, "is that the communicator is trying all the different possible tonal combinations to open this door. The problem is that there are, by my estimates, roughly 42,925 different possibilities."

There was a low moan from someone, probably Kodash.

"Gods," muttered K'Ehleyr. "It will take days to check them all through."

"Not really," replied Tania. "This is high-speed, remember. We've already gone through more than 8,000 combinations. Granted, we could be here for quite a while longer, but on the other h—"

Abruptly they heard a grinding noise.

They jumped back, startled at the racket. The door had suddenly started emitting a high-pitched, single tone. And somewhere beneath the ground, they heard the sounds of heavy gears, long unused, turning together.

"Back away!" Worf shouted. "Everyone!"

They did as he instructed. For one moment Worf wondered just how far would be safe. If somehow Tania had managed to trigger a self-destruct mechanism, then it probably wouldn't matter where they ran to.

"It's all right!" Tania was shouting over the noise. "It's all right!"

"How do you know?" demanded K'Ehleyr.

"It's my job to know!" Tania shot back.

The underground door had slid aside, and now something was rising. Everyone stared in amazement as a platform, with blinking lights set into its base, emerged. It clicked into place and waited patiently.

"It appears to be some sort of primitive turbolift," Soleta said.

"Maybe it's primitive," agreed Tania, "but it works. That's the important thing."

"All right," said Worf. "K'Ehleyr, myself, Soleta, Kodash, and Tania will enter. Mac, you will remain here and monitor our progress. We will leave a communicator with you so that we can keep in touch."

"Don't worry, Worf," said Mark. "Everything will be fine."

"I am sure it will be. All right, cadets." He gestured toward the raised platform.

"I mean, what's the absolute worst that could happen?" continued Mac. "The worst that happens is, we all die. And to die would be a great adventure."

They stared at him.

"Peter Pan said that," Mac told them. *"Peter Pan* is my favorite biography."

"Biography?" Tania looked blankly at him. "Mac, *Peter Pan* is fiction."

77

"It *is?*" He looked stunned. "Are you sure?"

"Yes!"

"Hmmm," he said. "This calls into question a number of my most basic beliefs. I'll have to think about this one long and hard."

"You do that," Worf advised him. "But keep aware of your duties as well."

"Not a problem."

Worf was the first one to step onto the platform. He balanced his weight on it for a second, as if to make sure that it was safe. When nothing unexpected happened, he gestured for the others to join him. They did so, crowding on and jostling for position. It was a tight squeeze.

"Now what?" Worf grunted, slightly crushed between Zak and Kodash.

Before anyone could reply, the floor suddenly jostled under them. With another grinding of unseen mechanisms, it sank downward, lowering them into the hidden base.

"Told you," said Tania smugly.

Mark McHenry watched them go. The moment they were out of sight, he tapped his communicator and said, "McHenry to Tobias. This is a test."

"We hear you, Mac," Tania's voice came back. "We're on line."

"Good." He nodded in approval. "Tania, a question. . . ."

"Go ahead."

"I don't suppose *Alice in Wonderland* was a travel guidebook, was it?"

"What?" came the surprised reply. "What did you say?"

"Oh, nothing. It's not important. I mean, who in his right mind would think that, right? Or would have parents who would tell him that, right?"

"Right," said Tania, sounding a bit uncertain about the whole conversation.

"Good. I—didn't think so. Let me know how it's all going."

"Will do."

He sat back and shook his head. "Mom, Dad, if I manage to get back, you have a *lot* of explaining to do."

CHAPTER

10

Tania sneezed violently, blowing dust off the wall.

"I'm sorry," she mumbled apologetically.

K'Ehleyr smiled slightly. "Yes, well, I would imagine that for some, the dust might be too much to . . ."

And then K'Ehleyr's nose twitched. She frowned, and then, unable to control it, sneezed. An even larger explosion of dust filled the air.

"Sorry," she muttered.

"It's all right," said Tania diplomatically.

Indeed, it was rather understandable. In fact, it was nothing short of amazing that more people weren't sneezing their heads off. The hidden base of the Brikar was not exactly the cleanest place.

The floors and walls were tiled, with elaborate mosaics built in. There was an array of images lining the wall that featured various Brikar in assorted poses of combat. Worf also picked out small pictorial representations of Klingons, Gorn, and various other races. The corridors were narrow, with intersections that appeared to jut out in different directions.

Right beneath his feet, he noticed a series of small gratings, spaced at about ten-foot intervals. But he had no clue as to what they were for.

"These pictures," Zak said, tapping the wall. "It is a history of the Brikar. This one, for example"—and he tapped one—"is a recounting of the Battle of Eldinsa'aar."

"Who? What?" asked Tania.

"The legend is that Eldinsa'aar—a mighty warrior—faced a horde of enemies, singlehandedly, in defense of a town that had only women and children left, for all the men had been slaughtered. Eldinsa'aar fought for twelve days and twelve nights, until the ground was so soaked with the red blood of the enemy that it was permanently stained red, and remains so to this day. The Eldinsa'aar Plains are named after him."

"We have similar legends," commented K'Ehleyr. "We speak of Kahless the Unforgettable—"

"Who battled his brother, Morath, for twelve days and nights, because Morath had broken his word," Worf said.

K'Ehleyr looked at him with interest. "It is good to know that you are aware of Klingon history."

"Of course I am," Worf told her. "Kahless has always been a great personal hero to me. I have endeavored to model myself on his example."

"As have I," said K'Ehleyr. Kodash, off to the side

and running his finger through the dust, nodded absently in agreement.

"It is interesting to observe," said Zak, "that there are certain fundamental philosophies we all share."

Kodash looked up. "I hope you are not implying, Brikar, that we might all become friends."

Looking disdainful, Zak replied, "Don't be ridiculous."

"Enough of this," said Worf briskly. "Tania—"

She was already studying the tricorder, but she was shaking her head. "Energy readings from all over the place. I'm having trouble locking any of it down. Anything could be anyplace."

"All right, then. We will just have to see what there is."

"Do we split up?" asked Soleta.

Worf thought about it a moment. "The main reason for dividing our forces would be to save time. I, for one, am in no particular hurry. I say we stay together."

"Logical."

"I am pleased you approve."

In the subspace monitor room, Gowr was trying not to nod off. He heard a scraping behind him, however, and that brought him to full and immediate attention.

He spun around in his chair to face the Brikar—

And saw, to his relief, that Baan was still exactly where he had been before. Still tied to the chair, his hands behind him.

"Is something wrong?" asked Baan casually.

"Nothing. Nothing at all."

"Well, that is a pity," said the Brikar. "You know, I think I shall make something be wrong."

His mouth was lopsided for a moment, and then abruptly he sent a wad of spit sailing through the air. It landed, with pinpoint accuracy, on Gowr's forehead.

Furious, Gowr was on his feet immediately, wiping the warm liquid from his face. "You Brikar slime!" he shouted, charging across the room. He had his fist drawn back, ready to slam the Brikar in the head.

He swung the fist forward—and Baan caught it.

It took a moment for Gowr to fully comprehend what had happened—that Baan's left hand was completely free, and was now clenching Gowr's own wrist in a merciless grip.

By that time, Baan had brought his other hand around from hiding. The strapping was still attached to it. With a quick snapping motion, he looped the strap around Gowr's throat.

Gowr tried to pull away, but he was unsuccessful. Baan gripped the other end of the strap with his free hand and drew it taut. Gowr was held fast, the strap choking off his air. He clutched desperately at his throat, trying to worm his fingers in between the strap and his skin. It didn't work.

Baan drew the strap even tighter, growling somewhere deep in his throat. "How do you like this, Klingon?' he snarled. "Eh?"

It was quite clear that Gowr wasn't able to hear him. His eyes rolled up into his head, and he slumped forward. His body went completely limp.

Baan held it a few moments more to make certain

that Gowr was dead. Then he released the straps, allowing Gowr's body to thud to the floor.

With his hands free, it only took him a few minutes to work his feet loose of their bonds. He left the straps, the chair, and Gowr's unmoving body behind him, and started across the compound to the generator building.

Worf stopped in front of one door and tapped the release button. The doors slid open obediently and Worf stepped in. Directly behind him was Tania, and she whistled. "I'm impressed," she said.

It was not a particularly large room, but a good deal had been crammed in. Most of it was of designs that were unfamiliar to Worf, but their intent was unmistakable. It was all weapons. And it was all nasty.

Worf took down one of the rifles from its clip on the wall and hefted it. Its muzzle was much larger than anything Worf had ever seen. It appeared to pack a respectable amount of fire power. "Solid," he said respectfully. "Good design. Good heft."

"You make a lovely couple," said K'Ehleyr. "Put it back."

Worf did so, albeit reluctantly. He made a mental note to himself to stop back there before they left and appropriate one of the firearms.

They stepped back out into the hallway. There was an intersection just ahead. More out of guessing than anything else, they decided to simply proceed straight ahead.

* * *

Mark McHenry dutifully kept an eye on things, which didn't seem to be all that much of a challenge. That, however, was about to change.

Mark felt, rather than saw, the shadow abruptly drop across him.

As detached and absorbed with irrelevancies as Mark's mind seemed to be at times, there was never anything slow about him when trouble presented itself. And his awareness of someone behind him brought a split-second analysis of the situation:

He knew that it wasn't Gowr, because Gowr was watching the prisoner and wouldn't abandon his post.

He knew that it wasn't someone to rescue them, because someone like that would have announced him- or herself in loud fashion before even entering the building. Shouts of, "Hello! We're from the Federation! Is anyone here?" would certainly have filled the air.

He knew it wasn't any of his fellow cadets because they, along with the other two Klingons, were still underground.

By process of elimination, it had to be Baan. Baan, apparently having escaped his imprisonment, overwhelmed Gowr, and was now standing directly behind him, quite possibly prepared to cave in Mark McHenry's head.

Mark had become somewhat attached to his head. Over the years, it had grown on him, and he had no desire to lose it.

All of this, as noted, went through his mind in less than an eyeblink.

Mark took immediate action. He lunged forward, and

was very much aware of air whipping just over his head, indicating that a powerful arm had just swung through the area that his skull had vacated.

He hit the ground and rolled, trying to put as much distance between himself and the Brikar as possible. He hit his communicator and shouted, "McHenry to Worf!"

Down below, Worf stopped where he was and tapped his comm badge. "This is Worf. Go ahead, Mac."

But before McHenry could get another word out, the Brikar connected with a backhand swing. Mark was fortunate that it was only a glancing blow.

It was, however, enough to render him unconscious. Mark collapsed in a heap on the floor.

Baan looked over his handiwork and smiled in approval. He figured that he should really kill McHenry as well, but that could wait.

What could not wait, he realized, was responding to Worf's voice. It was coming over Mark's comm badge, and the Klingon did not sound patient. "Mac, repeat, go ahead. What is it?"

Trying to buy time, the Brikar moved quickly. He picked up the comm badge, hesitated only a moment, and then said—in a fair approximation of McHenry's voice—"I forget."

It was exactly the right thing to say, for it drew an irritated sigh from Worf. "If you remember, contact us. Worf out."

"Yes, Worf out," murmured Baan with great satisfaction. "Worf, and Soleta, and all of you, are going to be out—for good."

CHAPTER
11

"What did Mac want?" Tania asked.

"Who knows." Worf shook his head.

Soleta, however, had overheard the brief exchange between Worf and McHenry and now returned to Worf's side. "I think something was wrong with him."

"Of course something is wrong with him. He lives in a world of his own."

"No, Worf," Soleta said firmly. "I detected a slight change in his voice. Also—and I would be the first to admit that Mark McHenry's mind does not move even in remotely logical fashion—simply contacting us and then forgetting why he did so . . ."

"That does sound a bit extreme," said Tania. "Even for Mac."

Worf looked from one of them to the other. The others had started to move ahead, but now K'Ehleyr returned to them. "What is going on?" she asked.

"I am not sure," he said. "But I believe I shall find out." He tapped his communicator and said firmly, "Worf to McHenry."

Baan was hunched over the tricorder and communicator rig that Tania had created. Mark's comm badge sat on the floor nearby. He heard Worf's voice come over it, but he was busy creating a specific series of code tones to be generated through the communicator.

The Brikar had, in fact, known precisely what tones would be required to activate the entryway. He had not been about to share that information with the cadets, of course.

He was also aware of other emergency back-up signals to punch in, booby traps and failsafes to be used in times of duress. This was definitely one of those times.

But here was Worf's voice again, and he didn't want to do anything that could tip the cadets before the trap was sprung. Well, he had bluffed his way through just before. He could easily do so again. After all, this was merely a Klingon. How difficult could it be to fool one of them?

"McHenry here. Go ahead."

Zak and Kodash ignored the discussion behind them and pressed on. They found a room where the door mechanism was not working properly and looked at each other for a moment.

"You interested in finding out what's in this room?" Zak asked.

"Of course."

Zak shoved his hands forward and managed to pry his rocklike fingertips into the crack. The moment he had it started, Kodash helped him pry it open.

When Zak peered in, it was all he could do not to shout out loud. "This is it," he whispered.

Sure enough, it was. In contrast to the general run-down look of much of the facility, the communications board was state-of-the art.

"We found it!" Kodash shouted. "K'Ehleyr! We found it!"

Then he heard Worf calling something back. Something about trouble.

That was when the rumbling started.

Kodash and Zak looked at each other, confused, and stepped back. The door, no longer being held open by them, hissed shut.

"What in Kolker's name is that?" said Zak uncertainly.

Moments earlier, Worf was speaking into his comm badge. "Mac, are you all right?"

"Fine," came the terse reply.

Worf glanced at the others for a moment. And then he said, "Mac, tell me about *Peter Pan.*"

There was the briefest of hesitations. "What?"

"Tell me . . . about . . . *Peter Pan.*"

The comm badge went silent.

Worf considered the possibilities, and knew in an instant. "The Brikar is loose. We are in great danger." Reflexively he yanked out his phaser, and shouted back over his shoulder. "Zak! Kodash! Trouble! Get moving!"

And then the ground started to rumble.

They looked at each other in confusion. "What's happening?" demanded Tania.

They staggered as the rumbling became more pronounced. From up ahead, Zak and Kodash were heading toward them, tottering as they came.

It was, naturally, Soleta who heard it first. She said one word, the significance of which Worf did not immediately understand. The word was "Water."

Baan set down the comm badge carefully, and then stepped on it. He smiled as he ground it into tiny metal scraps.

The Klingon had caught on. Baan grudgingly gave him credit for that. He had caught on, but it had come too late. The Brikar had managed to set the failsafe into operation, and the gentle rumbling beneath his feet told him that, very shortly, the cadets and the Klingons were not going to be a problem any longer.

Now they all heard it, a deafening roar. Worf pivoted to the left and then to the right, trying to figure out which way to go. His phaser was clutched tightly in his hand, but he wasn't sure which way to aim it, or what to aim it at.

And then it hit them.

A tidal wave, a torrential, onrushing cascade of water barreled toward them from either end. They barely had a second to react, and it wasn't nearly enough. Before they could even move, the water had hit them. They were knocked off their feet by the initial impact, and in the next moment they were swept upward. The impact was so violent that Worf's phaser was knocked out of his hand and washed away.

The push of the wave shoved them in one direction, only to be met by the water coming the other way. It slammed them around helplessly. Within seconds the corridors—with ceilings about five meters high—had been flooded. There was perhaps a meter of space at the top which the water had not yet filled, but more was being pumped in by the second and it wouldn't be long before there was no air left.

They tread water desperately, but they weren't able to hold their position because the water was now carrying them along in one direction so quickly. It was like being caught in the speeding rapids of a river. They would be pulled under, then shoved back upward like a cork to slam their heads against the ceiling before being dragged under once more.

Worf thrashed about underwater, trying to gain some sort of handhold somewhere, anywhere. Doors hurtled past him with incomprehensible speed. He reached out, trying to grab one to slow himself down.

And then he hit something.

He wasn't sure what it was, but he reacted immediately, grabbing on to it as if it were a life preserver. It took him a moment to realize that what he'd hit was a body. Underwater as he was, he couldn't make out who it was. But whoever it was had managed to find an anchor on something.

There was no way that Worf was going to risk dragging the person away from whatever safety had been found. But the anchored person seemed to be trying to encourage him to hang on.

Using his unknown savior as a ladder, Worf pulled himself up, inch by aching inch. The water hurtled past him, threatening to yank him loose, but Worf held on.

He pulled his head above the waterline and found himself literally nose to nose with K'Ehleyr.

"Hurry!" she grunted.

Worf saw that she was clutching on, with all her strength, to an overhead pipe that probably served as some sort of energy conduit. He grabbed it with one hand and then, when he was certain he had a firm grip, released her and clutched onto the conduit with both hands.

The water was up to their chins and rising.

"Any thoughts?" he asked.

"Yes," she grunted. "If I had known we would be dying so soon, I think I would not have wasted the time we had together."

He spit out some water, treading furiously to try and pull himself higher. "We are not going to die."

"You are being optimistic."

Worf looked around desperately. "No. I know what to do."

"Grow gills?"

"Right there," and he pointed. "That door there. Remember it?"

"What door? It's underwater!"

"That weapons room is behind there. If I can get to it—"

"You are crazy! Even if you can—"

"Look!" said Worf impatiently. "I can hang here and explain the whole plan, and drown in the meantime. Or I can try and get us out of this! Now do you want to complain or do you want to come along?"

K'Ehleyr sank slightly, and pulled herself back up. "Why not? I have nothing else planned for today!"

"All right! Here we go! One, two, three!"

On the count of three, he dove under. K'Ehleyr followed, not really expecting to make it back up.

Soleta, Tania, and Kodash splashed about furiously, trying to stay afloat. Zak was nowhere to be seen. The force of the water had slowed, but it was still rising.

Soleta started to sink, and Tania saw that Soleta was treading water only clumsily. Clearly she was not an experienced swimmer, and immediately Tania understood why. Vulcan was an arid, burning world. Swimming was simply not a major occupation on a planet with minimal moisture.

She tried to shout Soleta's name, but she swallowed water.

The Vulcan went under. And Kodash, weighed down by his heavy leather armor, sank too.

The push of the water almost shoved Worf right past the door he was trying to get to. But as he sailed past, his desperate fingers managed to snag the door frame.

K'Ehleyr was pushed down toward him. Bracing him-

self with his feet and one arm, he reached out with the other and managed to grab her before she went past.

Underwater, everything was silent. It was like being in the depths of space, except here they didn't have to worry about dying from explosive decompression.

Just drowning.

Worf managed to indicate that K'Ehleyr should push the "Door Open" controls situated in the wall near her. It was only at that moment he bleakly realized that if there was some sort of override in effect, the door would not open. In that case, they would never make it back to the surface, because Worf's desperate lungs were running out of air.

K'Ehleyr stretched her hand out, pushing against the flow of the water. Her fingers were inches short of the control pad. Worf gave her one additional shove, and her hand smacked against the pad.

The door obediently opened.

Worf, K'Ehleyr, and the water poured into the weapons room. It filled up within seconds, but for a brief second there was air. The two Klingons expelled what they had in their lungs and greedily sucked in more, a moment before being innundated once again.

At the Academy, the cadets had taken preliminary courses in weightless maneuvering, preparing for the possibility of being on a planet with lesser gravity than Earth's, or for the event of a ship's artificial gravity going out. Worf called those lessons to mind now.

He angled himself around underwater. He placed his feet against one wall and then pushed off, shooting across the submerged weightlessness of his environment. He sailed across the room and locked his hands onto the heavy-duty rifle he'd been examining earlier.

Even underwater, he could see K'Ehleyr's questioning look. *What good is that going to do?* it was asking.

He wasn't exactly in a position to explain.

He only hoped that his plan worked, and that the others would survive long enough to benefit from it.

Tania was pushed higher and higher toward the ceiling as the water rose.

Suddenly her feet hit something.

She couldn't tell what it was, and it didn't matter. It was something for her to stand on. She still had to fight the pull of the water with her arms, but at least she was able to brace herself.

And then Soleta bobbed to the surface on Tania's right. A second later, Kodash came up on the left. The water was up to their chins, even though they angled their heads back to draw in what little air there was.

"H—how . . . ?" Tania managed to gasp out.

Then she looked down. It meant submerging her head to get a better view, but she did it.

She was able to make out a form beneath the water—a large, humanoid form. She was standing on its head, and it was supporting the legs of the others with either arm.

She recognized it immediately.

Her head snapped back up and she managed to cough out, "Zak! It's Zak!"

Soleta, still expelling water from her lungs, managed to nod. Kodash was shaking his head, and even above the noise of the water Tania could hear him mutter, "Saved by a Brikar. I will never live this down."

Saved, however, was a wishful term. Clearly Zak was able to hold his breath for considerable periods of time, which was fortunate since he wasn't exactly built for swimming. But Tania knew he couldn't hold his breath forever.

And with the way the water was rising, even his support wouldn't help for too much longer.

With a scissor kick of his legs, Worf shot out into the corridor, holding the gun firmly. K'Ehleyr swam after him. She glanced up hopelessly, seeing the water rise closer to the ceiling, knowing that the end was near.

And Worf was playing with guns.

What was going through his mind?

Worf was hovering over one of the gratings on the floor, aiming the gun toward it.

That was when K'Ehleyr figured it out.

Worf squeezed the trigger.

A massive disruptor bolt ripped from the gun, straight down. Worf barely had time to be grateful that the weapon wasn't electrically based, since that might very well have electrified the water and fried both himself and K'Ehleyr. And then the force of the gun, due to the laws of action and reaction, shoved him upward with such force that he blasted out of the water and struck his head on the ceiling.

But he had guessed correctly: The grating was, in fact, part of a drainage system. Under ordinary circumstances, the water would have remained in place for a sufficiently long time to drown intruders. And then the drains would automatically open and the water would be emptied into an underground conduit, probably siphoned back into the holding tanks that had released it in the first place.

By blasting open one of the drain points, Worf had hurried the process along.

Grasping an overhead pipe, Worf watched. At first there was no sign of his having accomplished anything. But then the water below him started to swirl into a whirlpool.

K'Ehleyr.

Where was K'Ehleyr?

For a moment Worf had an image of K'Ehleyr being swept down into the underground water systems.

He was about to release his grip and dive down after her, when abruptly her hand emerged from the center of the whirlpool. She was fighting desperately against the pull of the water, and was clearly losing. Within seconds she would be pulled back down again.

She was beyond the reach of Worf's arm, but that wasn't going to stop him. He turned the rifle around and extended the butt toward her. Just before she was yanked under, she managed to grab onto it.

"Come on!" Worf shouted.

She brought her other hand up, clutching the rifle with full strength, and Worf dragged her toward him. His muscled arm twisted the rifle around and her head broke the surface. She sputtered water for a moment, and then with a fierce kick of her legs, drove herself upward so that she now had a grip once more on the pipe that was supporting Worf.

"It's—it's working!" she managed to say.

"Perhaps we can speed matters along," he rumbled. He shoved the disruptor underwater, angled it further up the corridor, and fired off several more shots. He hoped that his aim from memory was good enough to hit more of the gratings.

It seemed that it was. Another whirlpool started to form, and the water level was now very visibly sinking.

He twisted around, fired behind himself. A third whirlpool appeared. The tug of the water was fearsome, but they were solidly anchored on the overhead support.

"You did it!" she said.

"We did it," he replied, trying to sound modest. It did not suit him particularly well, though.

K'Ehleyr studied him a moment. And then she moved her head forward and, to Worf's astonishment, kissed him firmly.

"What was that for?" he asked.

She actually smiled, showing teeth, as she replied, "For me."

Tania didn't quite understand what had happened. All she knew was that one moment she had been fighting for the last bit of air, and the next moment the water level had dropped dramatically and was continuing to do so.

Within minutes she, Kodash, and Soleta were able to clamber down off Zak. He was standing there, smiling lopsidedly.

"That was pleasant," he said. "I can stay that way for a while longer, if you wish."

"I do not think that will be necessary," Soleta told him gravely.

"Come on," said Tania. "We've got to find Worf and K'Ehleyr—make sure they're okay."

"They are both Klingon," Kodash said firmly. "That is more than enough to ensure survival."

"Although having someone to stand on apparently does not hurt," Zak pointed out.

Kodash, wisely, said nothing.

Worf and K'Ehleyr waited until the water was only a foot or two deep, so low that they could clearly see the holes that Worf had blasted. When they finally released their grips, it was a bit of a drop.

They landed with a splash, crouching like panthers. Their hair was sodden and matted down, their clothes soaked through.

They were, however, alive.

"We have to get back up to the surface," said Worf. "Something obviously went wrong." He shouldered the disruptor. "But I think that we can handle it."

Baan didn't like what he was hearing.

Far below, he had detected what sounded, to him, like some sort of weapons discharge. And then something else, like water draining.

No, he didn't like it at all.

"What are they doing down there?" he snarled. Then he heard a low moan from across the room.

Mark McHenry was starting to sit up, rubbing his head and trying to pull his scattered wits together.

"Your people have ruined everything!" bellowed the Brikar.

Mac, still a bit confused, couldn't think of anything to say.

The Brikar advanced on him, his three-fingered hands curling into fists. "If they manage to get back up here, all they're going to find is your bloody corpse!"

There was a slight noise behind him. He started to turn, and then McHenry managed to take a breath and say, "You're about to get hit from behind."

This brought Baan's attention back to Mark. He sneered broadly. "What sort of pathetic trick is that—?"

Then he got hit from behind.

He went down from the impact to the nerve cluster on his back. The blow had caught him completely off guard.

He started to stand, and a vicious kick from a booted

foot snapped his head around, and he barely had time to see the enraged expression of Gowr.

Baan never got the chance to mount any sort of defense. He was having trouble recovering from the fact that Gowr was apparently still alive; that the raiders below had possibly managed to survive; that, in short, everything had gone horribly wrong. This, combined with Gowr's assault, left him hammered both physically and mentally.

By the time the Brikar slipped into unconsciousness, it was more merciful than anything else.

Gowr hit him a few more times even after the Brikar was out cold, for insurance. He looked over to Mac. "Are you all right?" he demanded. His voice sounded hoarse.

Mark nodded his head. "And you?"

"I have been better," admitted Gowr. Mark could see the cuts on Gowr's throat where Baan had endeavored to strangle him. "Fortunately, Klingon biology is very complicated. We have many internal back-up systems that non-Klingons are unaware of. We keep quiet about it; it makes it that much easier to surprise our enemies. We do not die quite that easily."

"I'm certainly convinced," said McHenry.

Then they heard a whirring noise, and the now-familiar sounds of hidden gears grinding. Seconds later the elevator platform rose, and a dripping wet exploration party came up from below. Worf was in the forefront, disruptor cradled in his arms. The others had obtained weapons as well from the weapons room. They were prepared for battle, for ambush, for anything except what they saw—namely, an unconscious Brikar on the ground, and Gowr and Mark in a casual conversation.

"Hi, guys," said Mark cheerfully. "Have you signaled for help yet?"

They looked at each other. "No," said Worf slowly.

"Well, maybe you'd better," Mark told them. "I don't think we want to hang around here forever, do you?"

Worf looked at K'Ehleyr. She shrugged.

"We will get right on it," Worf said.

"Good," said Mark McHenry.

CHAPTER
12

Everyone was seated around the conference-lounge table. They were looking up expectantly at Captain Taggert, the commander of the *Repulse*. At that moment, the *Repulse*—which had picked them up some hours earlier upon receiving their distress signal—was on the way to Starbase 3. There they would transfer to the vessel that would take them the rest of the way to Earth, to home, to the Academy.

"I hope you folks don't get too upset over this," Taggert began, scratching at his salt-and-pepper beard. "But it appears that you missed it."

Worf frowned, looking at the others. He spoke for all of them when he said, "Missed what, sir?"

"The so-called Brikar–Federation War. There have been some minor skirmishes the past few weeks. But the bottom line is that the Grand Alliance the Brikar thought they pulled together—an alliance between various races hostile to the Federation—has more or less fallen completely apart.''

"Why am I not surprised?" muttered Zak Kebron. "I could tell you stories about the fools running our government that would make your hair stand on end."

"That may very well be the case, Mr. Kebron. At any rate, they have been in touch with the Federation about settling differences via 'peaceful' means. Talks are being set up, although they will proceed with caution. The Brikar are claiming, though, that they have things to offer in return for various concessions of rights."

"What things?" Worf asked.

"Captives," said Taggert. "Various innocents who were en route to other destinations, and were captured by Brikar ships."

The cadets and Klingons looked at each other, and immediately they knew. "The colonists," said Soleta.

"Professor Trump," added Tania, referring to their injured Starfleet instructor who had left the planet with the others.

"That's right," said Taggert. "Our intelligence reports are that everyone is in good health. The Brikar are very much aware of the fact that dead captives will do them no good. We should be able to negotiate for their release with little or no problem. And considering that we have a ton of Brikar weaponry and a prisoner—thanks to you people—we'll have that much more additional leverage when it gets to talk.''

There was silence for a moment, and then Taggert said, "I want you people to know I am very impressed by the manner in which you handled things planet-side. Very impressed. And my comments and praise are going to be forwarded both to the Academy and to the Klingon Empire. You've acquitted yourselves admirably, and you are to be commended." He spread his hands and said, "I guess that's all. Dismissed."

Then a voice came over Taggert's comm badge. "Captain, this is Chafin. The Klingon cruiser *Azetbur* has dropped out of warp. They say they're here to pick up the Klingon team."

"Acknowledged." He turned to the young Klingons and said, "Better get your things and head over to the transporter. Wouldn't want to keep your people waiting."

K'Ehleyr nodded, and then looked at the Starfleet cadets. It was a moment that called for an impassioned speech, or perhaps a statement of thanks and appreciation for a job well done.

"Good-bye," said K'Ehleyr.

They rose as one and left the room.

The cadets looked at one another.

Worf sat immobile. There was a great deal he wanted to say to K'Ehleyr, but he didn't know quite how to begin, or even if he should.

Then he became aware of Tania watching him carefully, as if reading his mind.

Whatever emotions and thoughts were tumbling

through her own mind, she chose to keep them private. Instead, she slapped him on the shoulder and said, "Go after her, you fool."

The Klingons were entering the transporter room when K'Ehleyr heard a familiar voice shout from behind her. Gowr and Kodash paused, already in the open doorway. K'Ehleyr gestured for them to go on ahead, and then turned to face Worf.

He stood there a moment, still uncertain of what to say.

"So—what is your next assignment?" he said.

She looked a bit distant. "I have already applied to be part of the diplomatic team that would oversee the Federation–Brikar talks."

"You? A diplomat?"

Her eyes narrowed, but there was amusement in them. "Am I not the soul of diplomacy?"

"You are an elemental force, K'Ehleyr. Unstoppable. If diplomacy is what you have decided upon, then I have no doubt that you can force diplomacy down the throat of anyone who disagrees with you."

She laughed. Then, looking very serious, she said, "Worf, come with us."

He raised a questioning eyebrow.

"You are not one of them," she pressed on. "You are Klingon. You are one of us. Trying to fit yourself into their world—it is a waste. With them, you will always be an outsider. But with us . . ."

"I would be just another Klingon."

"Never," she said flatly. "The Klingon Empire would have much to offer you. And I . . ."

Her voice trailed off for a moment. For a moment she actually looked shy before she forced the imagined weakness from her and changed her tack. "It is not too late," she said.

He sighed, deeply, regretfully, but with a sense of conviction. "I have embarked on a path, K'Ehleyr. I must see that path through."

"You have no doubts?"

"I will always have doubts," he said. "But I will always overcome them."

She studied him and then said, "Perhaps you are a genuine Klingon, at that."

She stepped toward the transporter room, and Worf put a hand on her shoulder, stopping her. She looked at the hand, looked at him.

But their worlds were between them.

"Good life to you, K'Ehleyr," he said. "Face your foes bravely, and die honorably. I suspect we will not meet again."

"Good life to you, Worf," she replied. "Face your foes bravely, and die honorably." Then she paused, and added with a smile, "And I suspect—that you are wrong."

She reached into her pack and pulled out a small statue. She handed it to Worf. He recognized it immediately: It was a representation of Kahless the Unforgettable, locked in combat with Morath.

"Look at it any time you start to forget who you are."

And then she was gone.

Worf stayed outside the transporter room, his face immobile, until the whine of the transporter beams had faded completely.

Then he walked slowly away, cradling the statue, to seek the company of his fellow cadets from Starfleet Academy.

About the Author

PETER DAVID is a prolific author, having written in the past several years nearly two dozen novels and hundreds of comic books, including issues of such titles as *The Incredible Hulk, Spiderman, Star Trek, X-Factor, The Atlantis Chronicles, Wolverine,* and *The Phantom.* He has written several popular *Star Trek: The Next Generation* novels, including *Imzadi, Strike Zone, A Rock and a Hard Place, Vendetta,* and *Q-in-Law,* the latter three spending a combined three months on *The New York Times* bestsellers list. His other *Star Trek* novels include *The Rift* and *Star Trek: Deep Space Nine: The Siege.*

His other novels include *Knight Life* (a satirical fantasy in which King Arthur returns to contemporary New York and runs for mayor), *Howling Mad* (a send-up of the werewolf legend), the *Psi-Man* and *Photon* adventure series, and novelizations of "The Return of the Swamp Thing" and "The Rocketeer." He also writes a weekly column, "But I Digress . . ." for *The Comic Buyers Guide.*

Peter is a longtime New York resident, with his wife of fifteen years, Myra (whom he met at a Star Trek convention), and their three children: Shana, Guinevere, and Ariel.

About the Illustrator

Rocketed to Earth as an infant, JAMES FRY escaped the destruction of his home planet and grew to adulthood in Brooklyn, New York. After leaving Dartmouth College in 1979 he spent considerable time at the offices of New York Telephone and Merrill Lynch. In 1984, seduced by the irresistible combination of insane deadlines and crippling poverty, he embarked on a career as a freelance illustrator. James has created numerous characters and stress-related illnesses at both Marvel Comics and DC Comics. His greatest unfulfilled ambition is to get one full night of guilt-free sleep.